I0564191

OLLIE & BASH

On Cravenwood Block

A.D. ELLIS

A.D. ELLIS

ONE

Ollie Alexander Meyer

"DON'T MAKE IT OBVIOUS," I warned, sitting at a table in the Cravenwood diner, "but see that guy two tables over?"

My friend, Leighton, immediately craned his head, totally making it obvious. "The old guy?"

I scoffed. "He's not *old*, he's distinguished."

"Careful who you're calling old," my half-brother, Julian, said. "He looks right about my age."

I wrinkled my nose. "Nah, I'd say about forty."

Julian nodded. "Like I said, about my age. Thirty-five and forty aren't that far apart."

"Anyway, what about him?" Leighton asked, casting another look toward the man in question.

"He's hot, right?" I asked.

Julian snorted and Leighton shrugged. "I mean, I go more for tatted and dangerous looking..."

"Yeah, yeah, we know you've got a thing for the new tattoo artist on the block, but we're talking about me right now. You don't think the guy is hot?"

"He's a lot older than you," Julian said, ever protective.

"I'm twenty-four, not sixteen. Plus, this guy doesn't strike me as *old*. The new director I'm getting at work is *old*, probably wrinkly, bald, and decrepit. Hell, the words we've heard so far include *experienced*, *sophisticated*, and *seasoned*—like he's a fucking rotisserie chicken."

Julian chuckled in that quiet way he had—his caring, protective, quiet demeanor served him well as the apartment complex manager. He never got terribly up-in-arms about anything, just took life as it came. "Those words aren't synonymous with *ancient*, *elderly*, or *geriatric*. I'd just take it to mean the new director has a lot of experience and will be good for the education center."

I shook my head as our food was placed in front of us. "Whatever. Guarantee he walks with a cane, sports a comb-over, and probably has dentures." I waved off Julian's protest. "Back to hot guy. What do you think?"

"He's attractive," Julian conceded. "Not my type, but he definitely has appeal."

"He reminds me of a funky, old owl," Leighton said, picking lettuce, tomato, and onion from his burger. "And not *old* old, just funky, hipster...*wise* is the word I think I'm looking for."

"Why don't you just order your food the way you want it?" I asked, smiling at my friend, but completely agreeing with *funky, wise owl* to describe the hottie I'd been ogling across the diner.

"Just easier than asking for it without. It's no big deal to pick it off." Leighton shrugged.

"Wanna bet I can get his number and or suck him off

before the lunch rush is over?" I asked, already getting a thrill from the prospect of hitting on the guy and seeing where it could go.

Julian pinched the bridge of his nose. "Dear Lord, no," he grumbled, even as Leighton nodded enthusiastically. My brother shot an incredulous look between Leighton and me. "This is why the two of you should never be allowed together on your own. You're terrible influences on each other."

"Hey," I said, indignant. "I stopped Leighton from wearing booty shorts to the tattoo shop on his first trip there. That's gotta count for something."

Leighton nodded solemnly. "It's true. He did. But if my baby cakes tattoo hottie doesn't let me see how well he can use his gun soon, I'm gonna have to break the shorts out."

Julian scowled. "I thought you said the tattoo guy was straight?"

Leighton shrugged. "Pretty sure he is, but we're working our way to bestie status, and after that, the sky's the limit."

Julian closed his eyes and sighed. "We should pay the bill and head out."

"No, no, let me at least try to get his number." I slid from the booth. "Gimme five minutes."

"You go, girl," Leighton said, always my cheerleader. But Julian was right, Leighton and I were *not* a good combination when left on our own together.

I took a quick detour to the restroom just to check there was nothing in my teeth and my dark red hair—

seriously, with indoor lighting, it almost looked brown—was on point. Mischief stared back at me from deep brown eyes and I smiled. This guy wasn't going to know what hit him.

Striding confidently toward his table, I pulled the chair out, turned it around, and straddled it while giving him what I knew to be a sexy, flirty smile.

He looked up from whatever he was reading and scowled, glancing around the diner. "Um, may I help you?"

"You most definitely can. You see, I'm in desperate need of your phone number so we can get a date—or something similar—" I said with a wink, "set up soon." I pulled out my phone, ready to tap in his digits. "And I'm Ollie, by the way, just so you know what to moan when you're imagining me later."

The man studied me as if I was alien life speaking gibberish, leaned back in his chair, and crossed his arms over his chest. "Does that sort of crass behavior often work for you?"

"If you mean do I get plenty of digits and set up a fair number of *encounters*, yeah, for sure." I wiggled my phone. "Don't leave me hangin', man."

"Look, Oliver," he began.

"It's Ollie."

"Oliver seems more like a child who is acting out and needs reprimanded." He raised his brow. "And if the shoe fits."

I narrowed my eyes, suddenly not as in love with my funky, wise old owl.

"I'm new on Cravenwood Block. I have a new job plus

a plethora of other *adult* responsibilities to keep me busy. Even if I were the type of guy to hand out my *digits* during lunch at a diner, I wouldn't give them to a man who appears to be half my age." His expression softened. "I'm flattered, really, but it's going to be a no for me."

Pursing my lips, obsessing a bit over his rough-edged voice, and realizing the twitch of my dick came from how hot the idea of a challenge made me. "I'll admit defeat. For now. But if you're new around here, I bet we see more of each other. I'm a hard guy to say no to." I leaned in. "And I promise to make it very worth your while."

I licked my lips and stood, giving him a little nod as I made my way back to Julian and Leighton.

Leighton grimaced. "Did that feel as cringey as it looked?"

Julian covered a laugh with his hand and pretended to cough.

"What? No, just a reminder to up my game." I took a long drink of water. "Boys, that man *will* be in my bed—literally or metaphorically speaking—before too long. Maybe not today, maybe not tomorrow, but..." I paused so Leighton could join in. "There's never a shortage of men wanting to shove their dicks down your throat," we chorused together, laughing.

I shrugged. "I just have to figure out how to get *that* dick," I pointed toward where my guy sat, "down *this* throat."

Julian groaned. "And with that, I'm leaving. Somehow, you two always make clogged drains, sticky windows, and squeaky exhaust fans sound good."

The three of us made our way to the front to pay and I gave a wink to my guy.

Sure, he seemed a bit standoffish and stuffy, but he was new to town and probably overwhelmed. All I had to do was see him again and make it known I was ready, willing, and able to help him blow off some steam.

Julian headed back toward Cravenwood Apartments.

Leighton beelined toward Cravin' Ink Designs where he'd latched onto the hot artist who owned the place. Jett Nelson had no idea what he was in for with Leighton.

I made my way back to my apartment, but took the long way in hopes of clearing my head as I traveled around Cravenwood Block. The name of the community within a community, located on the west side of Midtown, was always good for a few laughs, especially among a group of gay men living together. I mean, weren't we all *cravin' wood*?

Immature?

Maybe.

But it still made me laugh.

I hadn't lived in Cravenwood for very long, but Julian had made it his mission to learn the history of the place before he took the job managing the Cravenwood Apartments. As far as my understanding of our little community went, about twenty-five years earlier, a man named Robert Cravenwood got pissed about a proposed demolition of buildings which would make way for a parking garage. Mr. Cravenwood—seriously, what bad luck for a last name—anyway, he bought the buildings and the land. Leighton liked to joke that Robert must have been a sugar daddy, but I digress. He restored a few buildings, rebuilt a few, and brought the area back to life. I wasn't sure if he named it after himself or if people just started using his name for the area, but Cravenwood was born. It wasn't a town, but the city of Midtown named the street running down the middle of the block Cravenwood Avenue and many of the businesses used Cravenwood or *cravin'* in their name.

As if I was in a documentary, my thoughts played out as I passed the Cravenwood Health Center and Cravin' Cuts.

Leighton worked at Cravin'-a-Cup as a kickass barista.

I worked as the music department head at the Cravenwood Education Center.

The area referred to as Cravenwood Block was like a little bubble inside a bubble. Midtown wasn't a super large city, it bordered between a large town and small city, but living and working in Cravenwood seemed to make everything feel smaller, safer, and more connected.

A lot of people who worked on Cravenwood Block also lived here, and I'd lucked out with landing both a job *and* an apartment, thanks in part to my brother being manager of Cravenwood Apartments.

When he'd taken over the apartment complexes—which were Cravenwood Apartment Tower A and B, both three-floor buildings stretching the entire length of the block. CAT A on the westside and CAT B on the eastside, the towers facing each other—Julian took CAT A and assigned his assistant, Chloe, to CAT B.

The best thing Julian ever did with the towers—okay, let's all just agree three-story buildings aren't exactly towers, but there are bigger problems in the world—

anyway, the best thing he ever did was designate a huge portion of the third floor on both towers to being residences for Cravenwood Block workers.

Maybe it was because I worked on the block. Maybe it was because Julian was my brother. Maybe a combo, but I'd lucked out with one of the top-floor living spaces.

While Julian did a great thing reserving space for Cravenwood Block employees, there wasn't much he could do for the set-up of the employee apartments. However, living so close to where I worked allowed me— and most others—to overlook the uniqueness.

There were three employee residences—each with room for eight individuals—on each tower. Employees on Cravenwood Block *could* opt for other apartment spaces, but they'd definitely lose out on the perk of top-floor living.

The top-floor apartments in both towers had private access to the rooftop pool, dining area, sauna and jacuzzi, gym, and lounge area.

The living space of each employee residence was designed to have a living room, a kitchen, a laundry, four double-occupancy bedrooms sharing two bathrooms, and an additional half bathroom near the laundry room.

The bedrooms were the unique part.

Whoever originally designed the space must have thought a lot of adults living on their own wouldn't want to share a room like kids in a dorm, so the bedrooms had one door that opened to a shared little foyer or lounge-ish area, and then each sleeping area had its own door. The sleeping area had room for a queen-sized bed, dresser, and desk. There was a built-in closet and each room shared a bathroom with the neighboring room through the lounge area.

Hypothetically, a couple could share one sleeping area, but the living-space would get really crowded if there were sixteen people rather than just eight. Maybe a couple here and there would be okay, but so far, we'd never had more than eight people living in our apartment.

The Cravenwood Tap sign caught my eye down the block. It was smack-dab next to the education center— something a few parents wanted to complain about, but it wasn't as if we were taking the kids for shots during naptime. I could have made my way to the center and worked on a couple things, but I was truly dreading meeting the new director, so I cut my walk short and headed upstairs to my room.

Maybe a trip to the Tap the next night would help me forget about the anxiety of getting a new boss.

Yeah, that was exactly what I needed.

"Leighton?" I hollered from the doorway of my room hoping he was back from pestering Jett during work hours.

My gray-eyed, blond-haired, sunshiny friend popped out of his door. "You rang?"

"You wanna help me pick out clothes for the Tap?"

His brows shot up. "You're going to the Tap right now? I mean, I guess it's five o'clock somewhere."

I laughed. "No, tomorrow night. Wanna come?"

"Nah, I'll help you get gorgeous, but I wanna have time to hang out with Jett."

"Does Jett know you have a hang-out date?" I teased.

"Not yet, but when I show up and charm him with my winning personality, he won't mind."

I sighed. "I hope you know what you're doing with that one."

"It's all good," Leighton promised.

"You thought Stephon was all good too," I reminded him. Counseling had helped me figure out some of my own past shitty baggage, and I often found myself wanting to save my friends from heartache and hurt—but in reality, I knew we all were adults and it was probably best to learn from our mistakes. Still didn't mean I wanted my friends diving into sucky situations.

"Hush, we don't need to speak of him. I like Jett—as a friend first and something more only if he's down, which he probably never will be—and I enjoy spending time with him." Leighton gestured toward my room. "Now, what kind of vibe are you hoping to give off tomorrow night?"

"Hot, sexy, down-to-to-fuck-or-at-least-suck, but nothing too desperate."

Leighton grinned and clapped his hands before tearing into my closet.

Down-to-fuck may have been a slight exaggeration. Don't get me wrong, I was definitely down, I just maybe didn't have *as* much experience with sex as I let on. I'd kissed *a lot* of guys. I'd been on the giving and receiving end of *a lot* of head.

Beyond that—

"Hey, how about these jeans?" Leighton interrupted my thoughts.

"I like those, but what shoes and shirt?" I let him pull me into a whirlwind of fashion for the next hour.

The next night, I'd dull the anxiety of a new boss with some drinks and hopefully a sexy guy.

Monday, I'd face the work situation.

And I'd definitely keep an eye out for my funky, wise owl.

He might not have taken the bait right away, but I wasn't one to give up so easy.

TWO

Sebastian "Bash" Thomas Evans

ALL I WANTED to do was crash in bed and sleep for a week.

I snorted as I tucked the receipt from the diner into my pocket and headed toward the rented moving truck. I'd come to Cravenwood Block for lunch on a whim, hoping for a break from moving my entire life from my university-owned townhouse into a storage facility nearby.

I'd lived on the east end of Midtown for nearly a decade.

Moving across town to Cravenwood on the west side had *not* been on my agenda—not that the area wasn't great, I just hadn't planned on moving.

Instead of taking my mind off the job situation which had necessitated the move, lunch on Cravenwood Block had thrown me for a loop.

And the loop was a certain way-too-young man named Ollie with dark red hair and dark brown eyes.

At forty-two, I should have been completely put-off by the kid's behavior at the diner.

And I was.

Except...

For some reason, I couldn't stop thinking about him.

Not so much about his request for my number and insinuated proposition, just about *him*. What made him smile? Where did the confidence come from? Was it hiding something? Who did he call friends? What did he like to do?

Driving back to the townhouse in hopes of only one more load to take to the storage garage, I tried my best to think of something other than Ollie or the whole reason I had a new job anyway.

While I maybe hadn't been in love with my old job at the university—sure, I'd liked it well enough, but I'd been planning to leave it soon anyway—I was pissed and embarrassed at the reason I'd been forced to leave.

I could have fought it—and likely would have won—but I wasn't keen on getting my name run through the mud any more than it already had been. After the allegation, I'd been grateful the university had let me resign quietly. When the young man who'd made the accusation was caught in his lie, part of me wanted to go back and demand they give me back my job. But rumors had already spread. I'd already resigned. And leaving had been in the back of my mind prior to the shitshow anyway.

So, I'd followed through.

The new position on Cravenwood Block had basically fallen in my lap. At first, I'd been hesitant to take a job I was overqualified for, but I'd convinced myself it would be a bit of a break while I looked for something else.

The new job came with some perks—the biggest of which being I was closer to LuLu—and was just a blip on the map of my career. I'd build up my experience and successful background at the new job while looking for a position that would challenge me and engage my qualifications.

In other words, I had no plans to be on Cravenwood Block for long.

But for the time being, I'd deal with it.

The first order of business was to find a place to live. I needed to be *on* Cravenwood Block for work, and renting a vehicle—even just for moving loads to the storage unit—was stupid expensive. So, it made the most sense to attempt to find a place on the block.

I hoped to simultaneously get settled in at work and find a place I could rent month-by-month or at least do a six-month lease.

And if I could save up some money for LuLu during this time, all the better.

As I heaved box after box into the moving truck, I tried to push Ollie from my head. I needed to think of anyone but that kid.

Randal's face popped into my head.

Fuck.

No.

I definitely didn't want to think about Randal.

Fifty-five to my forty-two, Randal had been my first real relationship—everyone before had been fun, but nothing serious.

We'd met when I was thirty-five, fucked around for a couple years before I realized I was the *other* guy. At thirty-seven, I'd been thrilled—and blind—when Randal left his long-time boyfriend to be with me.

We'd had nearly four good years together proving cheaters can reform and age gap romance can work.

Until I walked in on him with his pool boy.

We'd broken up, obviously, and Randal had moved on easily.

He was now married to the pool boy, Oscar. They had twins. Oscar stayed home with the babies. Randal made enough money to hire another pool boy. And they seemed truly happy.

Only a tiny part of me hoped Randal would cheat *again* and prove it wasn't just because I hadn't been enough.

No, I definitely didn't need to think about Randal.

Ollie's deep brown eyes popped into my head.

Nope.

Not going there.

A pretty young man with blue eyes and curly black hair flitted through my head.

God, no.

He was even worse than thinking about Randal or Ollie.

Caleb.

The whole reason for my current situation.

He'd been in one of my university classes—an intro to elementary education for second-semester freshmen—and had been an unabashed flirt.

The day after I'd found Randal begging Oscar to fuck him harder—yeah, I should have taken a personal day, but hindsight and all that—I'd clearly been *off* in class.

Caleb had hung around after class and turned the flattery and flirting up several notches.

At any other time, I would have politely told him I wasn't anywhere close to interested and sent him home. However, that particular day, my guard was most definitely down.

It still made me angry I hadn't recognized the manipulative gleam in his eyes when I finally came to my senses and shut it down—had I been in a better headspace, I would have gone directly to my superiors and told them what happened.

As it was, I'd thought sending him on his way with a firm *this isn't going to happen* was enough.

It wasn't until the allegation came to light that I realized my error.

Weeks of closed-door meetings and mediation finally led to me taking the offer to resign and walk away.

Finding out later Caleb had been caught in his lie and everything had unraveled like a cheap sweater had helped, but it hadn't been enough.

I pushed Caleb out of my head—the kid had falsely accused me and could have cost me my career. As it was, my attorney and Caleb's parents' attorney had worked out some form of restitution I'd refused to be any part of—as in, I didn't even want to know the smallest detail other than the monetary deposits into my bank account and knowing it had been made clear to Caleb that he never contact me.

Ever.

That left me with my new job, LuLu, or Ollie to think about.

As much as I loved LuLu, those thoughts also brought anxiety.

I wasn't nearly excited enough for the new job—was it bad I truly felt above it?

Damn it.

Ollie.

Why couldn't I get that kid out of my head?

Arriving at the storage facility, I made quick work of unloading the truck.

Within the hour, I had the rental returned and was in the back seat of an Uber heading *back* to Cravenwood Block.

I'd take a walk, see the area, and at least get my office set up before I went back to an empty townhouse to live out of a duffle bag for two more nights. After that, I'd either need to have an apartment or get a hotel room for a while.

Opting to set up my office first, I let myself into my new building. Turning on a true crime podcast, I went to work organizing before taking a brief self-guided tour of the place.

I'd been assured the business ran smoothly and the employees were the best.

Which was promising because, despite all of my qualifications and years of experience, I'd never run an entire organization by myself. Sure, I'd kept high school and college students in line during my years in the classroom, but I'd never actually been anyone's boss.

Later, as I walked around Cravenwood Block, doing my best to be excited for a new challenge rather than defeated thanks to the actions of others, I took in the businesses.

I knew the diner was delicious.

I had a feeling Cravin'-a-Cup would be a favorite.

It was nice to know I wouldn't have to go far for a haircut.

I'd definitely get a membership at the gym.

I groaned inwardly, but it was nice to know I could have a doctor so close.

And I made plans to stop into the flower shop to buy bouquets for all my new employees the following week.

When I saw Cravenwood Tap, I immediately wanted to pop in for a drink.

But I also just wanted to go home to bed.

I argued with myself for a while and opted to go home, but decided I'd come check out the bar the next night if the pull was still there.

Ordering an Uber—and truly wishing I already lived on Cravenwood Block—I headed back to my empty townhouse.

THREE

Ollie

_____

I LOST myself on the dance floor.

Leighton had styled me and I was feeling good after our bonding time. I was worried about him getting involved with Jett—or more like getting hurt by Jett. Leighton had been hurt in the past and I didn't want to see it happen again.

Julian had reminded me Leighton was a grown-up and could make his own decisions, but that didn't mean I wanted my friend hurt.

Speaking of my brother. He'd seemed preoccupied about his prospective new roommate. Actually, there was talk of three new roommates, a ridiculous hint of Leighton possibly offering Jett a room, and Julian seemed a bit flustered. I'd need to chat with him to see what was up.

But for the time being, I was happy to drink and dance as I attempted to forget about the fact my new director started tomorrow. Why couldn't Elise have stayed? She was really good. She let us do our jobs, didn't micromanage, and trusted us as professionals.

I bet the new guy was the micro-est micromanager who ever micromanaged.

Okay, yeah, to say my anxiety was on high over getting a new boss was an understatement.

I returned my attention to the music and almost-empty glass in my hand. Taking a short break, I headed toward the bar.

Lucas, one of Cravenwood Tap's best bartenders made amazing drinks. He was actually one of the rumored potential roommates, but things weren't completely finalized—and I wasn't sure he even knew I was Julian's brother—so I didn't even bring it up to him when I ordered another Liquid Marijuana as the music thumped.

Cravenwood Tap wasn't a gay bar, but it had a decent mixture of folks and a welcoming atmosphere. Cravenwood was a lot more progressive than the whole of Midtown—and even Midtown was considered fairly liberal —which was only one of many things this particular gay boy appreciated about where I lived.

The Tap did a good job of rotating theme nights with the music they played and drinks they served. And the friendly servers and easy-going crowds were always a plus.

Lucas handed over my sweet and fruity drink—awww, sweet and fruity just like me—and I contemplated how many more I could have before the hangover from hell would haunt me the next day. With a wink and thank you, I headed back toward the dance floor.

But I stopped dead in my tracks.

It was him.

My funky, wise owl guy from the diner.

Sitting at a high-top table in the corner.

Alone.

Nursing what appeared to be a whiskey sour or similar.

I smiled and sent up a thank you to the gods of gay boys or fate or *whoever* had placed this fine man back in my path.

It was a sign.

Right?

It had to be a sign.

A sign for me to try, try, try again.

Taking a long, fortifying sip of my drink, I headed straight for his table.

Goals were important.

My mini-goals included getting his name and his number.

My swing-for-the-fences goal included his dick down my throat in the bathroom before I headed home.

But I was willing to work up to that.

As far as long-term goals went, I definitely wanted a date with the man. Which was weird for me, I usually just stuck to quick and easy encounters and moving on. Dating hadn't really been my thing in the past.

But this guy...

True, I knew next-to-nothing about the man, but something about him intrigued me.

His dark, serious eyes.

That stylishly floppy brown hair.

The neatly trimmed, hipster-vibe facial hair that bordered just between sexy scruff and full-on beard.

He was taller than me, I was sure. I hadn't seen him standing up, but I was only five-seven so a lot of people were taller than me.

He had the type of body designers probably loved because he was tall and lean and likely looked good in whatever he wore.

Tonight, he'd opted for designer, dark-wash jeans and a button-up with subtle vertical stripes. A bit dressier than the Tap usually got, but he looked good.

"Hey there," I said over the music as I climbed onto the tall chair. "Fancy meeting you here. Seems like if we're going to be running into each other on the block, I might as well have your name and number."

He stared at me, smirked, shook his head, and took a sip of his drink. "Oliver."

I pursed my lips. "It's Ollie."

"Sebastian, but I prefer Bash," the man said.

I had a name. Goal number one complete. "Hi, Sebastian who prefers Bash, but insists on calling me Oliver instead of Ollie. Nice to meet you properly. What brings you out tonight?"

He snorted before draining his glass and catching the eye of one of the servers. "Another whiskey sour and whatever *Ollie* is drinking, please."

The woman studied my drink. "Liquid Marijuana?"

"You're good." I'd drained the drink in my hand way too quickly, but I wasn't going to turn down my new friend buying me another.

She smiled and headed to get our drinks.

"Thanks," I said. "Now, what brings you out tonight?" I'd immediately noticed he was much looser than he'd been at the diner and assumed the drink had something to do with it.

"A shit run of bad luck brings me out tonight, my dear Oliver," Bash answered, staring remorsefully at the ice swirling in his glass.

As much as I'd never really cared for people calling me Oliver, I couldn't bring myself to even care when Bash did it because I was just happy he was talking to me. And honestly, *Oliver* sounded sexy-as-fuck in his rough-edged voice—kinda like a smoker's, but I hadn't caught a whiff of tobacco and his teeth were brilliantly white, so I doubted he actually smoked.

"Well, that sounds like a story."

"Not one you want to hear," Bash said.

"Try me."

"Not one I want to tell," he said stubbornly.

I paused as the server brought our drinks and Bash closed out his tab. "Talking is a good way to work out what's bothering us. Or we can venture to the bathroom and I can take your mind off that shit run of bad luck." I waggled my brows. "Or both."

Bash stared at me for several moments and huffed. "The fuck is wrong with me?" he muttered. "Swear the universe has it out for me." He closed his eyes and breathed deeply as if trying to calm himself.

"I choose to believe you don't mean *I'm* a punishment from the universe," I quipped, only slightly offended.

Bash's eyes popped open and he sighed. "No, not you. Just...situations."

"I'm a good listener." I leaned closer, completely sincere and not the least bit ashamed. "And I'm even better on my knees. Just so you know. If that's something you'd be interested in."

Bash snorted. "Why am I not running far, far away from you?"

I winked and shrugged while sipping the pale green liquid through my straw. "I'm pretty and engaging and you can't help thinking about what your dick might look like between my lips."

"Fuck," Bash mumbled, glancing around to see if anyone had heard what I'd said. But we were tucked in a far corner and it wasn't like I'd yelled the words. "First, I find out I'm the *other man*," Bash said, as if resigning himself to my listening ear. "Then I find out once a cheater, always a cheater when I walk in on the pool boy fucking my boyfriend. Then one mistake turns into an accusation that cost me my job." He pinched the bridge of his nose while he muttered. "And now fate puts this gorgeous man who is much too young for me in my path as if testing to see if I'm smart enough to say no or stupid enough to miss my chance."

I whistled, only slightly preening over the fact he'd called me gorgeous. "Damn, yeah, that sounds like a shit run of bad luck for sure. All of that," I gestured vaguely in regards to the words he'd spoken, "happened recently?"

Bash took another sip and stared at me over the rim of his glass.

For a moment, I truly thought he was just going to ignore the question.

But he sighed and shook his head. "No, over the past few years. Finding out I was the other man should have been the end of that whole situation, but I thought the fact he left the guy for me meant it was something real."

I winced. "Finding him fucking the pool boy proved differently, huh?"

Bash snorted. "Something like that."

"And the false accusation?"

He took another drink and stared into the amber liquid. "More recently and the whole reason I'm on Cravenwood Block." His dark eyes met mine. "And I'm wondering if there's something wrong with me because this," he gestured between us, "feels a little too much like that same situation all over again."

The frown on my face wasn't a cute attempt at flirty or suggestive. "I'm not exactly sure what that means, but if you're insinuating I'm the type to make false accusations, you can go fuck yourself." I leaned in. "I think you're hot. I'd be happy to suck you off and make you forget your problems for a while. If you're going to be around here, I'd even venture as far as to suggest maybe we get together from time to time." The sound of my knuckle tapping the table drew his attention for a moment. "But if you're suggesting I'd make up lies about you to either get my way or because I didn't get my way…"

Bash held up a hand. "No, I'm sorry. That wasn't my intention. I don't know you at all, I have no right to suggest you're anything like him. I'm just questioning my own sanity right now."

"What did he do?" I was beyond buzzed and definitely would feel the effects in the morning, but nothing could have pulled me away from Bash at that moment.

He opened his mouth, but clamped it shut. "Don't really want to rehash it tonight. Suffice it to say I was at a low point, fell for his flirting, stopped things before they got too far out of hand, and he didn't handle the rejection well."

I bit my lip. "Since we don't know each other and I'd rather offend you now than later when we're dating or in bed, may I ask…" I trailed off and waved a hand. "You know what, never mind, that was rude and not my place."

Bash snorted. "You've offered to suck me off multiple times, I think rude and not your place is kinda your thing."

I pressed a hand to my chest in mock shock. "Excuse me? I prefer to think of my personality as *up front* and *engaging*."

Bash chuckled—the alcohol had definitely loosened him up. "If you were going to ask about his accusation—I swear it was false. He got caught in the lie a bit later, but the damage was already done. He was over-age, the little bit we did do was consensual—even more so on his part than mine—and the rest he made up as revenge because I stopped things and turned him away." He smiled sadly. "I'm not one to take advantage; I prefer my partners to be willing, enthusiastic participants."

My eyes went wide as I grinned.

Bash pushed his drink to the side. "Annnnd, I've clearly had more than enough to drink and just need to shut up."

"Willing and enthusiastic, huh? Well, let me just tell you about how willing and enthusiastic I can be."

He rolled his eyes with a huff. "You're like a damn dog with a bone. I need you to know I'm not here for long, six months to a year at the most."

I pursed my lips. "Well, that kinda puts a damper on my plan to lure you into a happily ever after. I'll cancel the wedding invitations and photographer." When Bash narrowed his eyes, I continued. "Look, I'm talking about a blowjob if you're down and maybe a few possible dates here and there. I can be a lot of fun. It's not like I'm asking to move in with you and have you put me on your health insurance or get a key to your safe deposit box."

Bash chuckled darkly. "Good for you, since you'd be shit out of luck."

I let the comment go, not exactly sure what he meant other than maybe alluding to something about money.

"So, how about you give me your number and we meet in the bathroom for five minutes of fun?" I waggled my brow.

Bash ran a hand over his face. "I'm probably going to regret this for multiple reasons, but I'm going to give you my number and say goodbye. I can't start a new job around here and risk getting caught in a compromising position in the men's room." He shocked the shit out of me when his hand covered mine. "And you are worth more than five minutes on your knees."

I swallowed thickly, a weird sensation washing over me—I had some baggage and had definitely never had a man telling me I was worth anything more than fun—but I pushed it aside and pulled out my phone. Bash rattled off his number and I assigned him to my contacts before texting him.

Save this number. -Ollie

Bash chuckled and tapped his phone screen a few times before turning it around and showing me he'd assigned me as *Oliver* in his contacts.

"So, um, thanks for the drink." I slid from the tall chair. "Guess I better head home, be a responsible worker, and get some sleep and all that."

Despite not being able to get up close and personal with Bash, I wasn't upset. In fact, I really wanted to ask him to walk to the park with me and spend hours chatting, but I needed to sleep off the alcohol and get to work on time the next day.

Even though I wasn't thrilled to be getting a new director, I still wanted to make a good impression—and it wasn't as if I had any control of whoever the owner put in charge.

"Thanks for the company," Bash said, his hand on my back as he led me out the door. That warm sensation overtaking me again—had any guy ever touched me and treated me like I mattered?

No. Not once.

To be fair, I'd never given any guy a reason to think I was into him for anything but fun—always leaving long before anything could go very far—but Bash's protective hand on my back was a completely new experience.

I wanted more.

And I wasn't one to go looking for more.

My usual pattern was find a hot guy, make out, get off with him, and either purposely push him away or not be upset when he lost interest before anything got too serious.

I was a serial maker outer and blow jobber…yes, I was very well aware those weren't real words, but let's just go with it.

If guys didn't want to stick around—whether by choice or because I conveniently lost their number—that just allowed me to discover more fish in the sea and all that.

But Bash had me thinking about dating and walks in the park and hands on the small of my back.

Bash was different.

Pulling myself from the unsettling, yet not completely unwanted thoughts, I glanced up and down the block.

"Which way are you?" I asked.

"Oh, I'll have to call a ride. I don't live on or even near the block just yet. That's on my list of things to do."

I couldn't help the butterflies fluttering in my gut as a warmth overtook me.

See, I knew meeting Bash was fate.

"You're kidding, right?"

Bash cocked a brow. "Not in the slightest. I just moved all of my stuff to a storage facility and I hope to find something around here soon."

"The alcohol has my head all fuzzy, so now isn't the best time for details, but make sure we talk. The apartment I live in has at least one room available to rent." I leaned in and kissed Bash's cheek, not a bold move for me, but more heartfelt than any move I'd made on a guy in the past. "Since I couldn't entice you with a bathroom BJ, maybe I can pull you in with an apartment."

Bash's body tensed and I *felt* the moment of indecision

where he wanted to pull me close—and maybe do dirty things to me—but he huffed out a breath and stroked a hand down my arm.

"You're entirely too young for me, but I'm beginning to think maybe there really was a reason we ran into each other—for someone so young, you're definitely the most genuine and intriguing man I've met in a very long time. I've got to get home and sleep, got a million things to do tomorrow, but can I text you about the apartment details?"

"Definitely. And maybe we can set up a date, too?" I shrugged. "Bathroom BJs are always an option—other locations available too—but a date with a funky, wise owl sounds delectable." I was out of my league, but a tiny voice in my head told me to take a chance with this man.

Bash cocked a brow. "A what?"

I chuckled. "Just go with it." Leaning in, I kissed his scruffy chin. "Sleep tight."

I felt Bash's eyes watch me until I disappeared around the corner, and you're damn right I made sure my ass looked its best as I walked away.

Once showered and in bed for the night, the alcohol keeping me warm and a bit hazy, a huge smile filled my face as I thought of the prospect of Bash moving in.

Yeah, yeah, it was presumptuous and I was definitely getting ahead of myself.

But I couldn't help it.

At least *thinking* about it.

Remember the apartment set-up? Four *rooms* each with a main door, a foyer or lounge area, a shared bathroom, and two sleeping areas behind separate doors, right?

Well, the four main doors were green, orange, purple, and blue.

I knew Lucas and his best friend, Dean, had already spoken up to share a main room which meant they'd be behind the green door. Julian had one of the rooms behind the orange door and seemed pretty set on Dean's work friend, Shaw, moving in with him—I didn't know many details, but Julian already appeared dang protective of Shaw.

That left the purple door and the blue door.

Leighton was behind the purple door and there was no way he'd accept Bash living with him if he was still hoping for Jett to move in.

So really, even if I didn't fight for it too hard, the spare room behind the blue door—sharing with me—was really Bash's only option.

Sure, there were maybe some rooms in the other building, perhaps even on our floor, but I was pretty sure I could convince Julian to sell Bash on sharing a room in *our* apartment.

Maybe I hadn't gotten the type of action I was hoping for that night, but if that disappointment led to *living with* Bash, it was well-worth it.

Delayed gratification and all that.

Maybe I was turning a corner, growing up, discovering new things about myself because the old Ollie didn't delay gratification. The old Ollie didn't get excited about a crush potentially becoming a roommate.

I fell asleep with a smile on my face, not even once worrying about the new director taking over the education center the next day.

I was sure he'd be just as horrible, old, and hateful as I'd been imagining, but the thought of Bash contacting me about a place to live was enough to push the negative image away.

———

THE NEXT MORNING, I was delighted to wake up and find my head only slightly throbbing from way too many sweet drinks the night before.

After popping some pain relievers, I showered and fixed my dark red hair before pulling on distressed black jeans, a black t-shirt, and a dark gray cardigan since the morning would be crisp and cool—and the center was known for being on the chilly side most of the time.

I truly did love my job. Music was something that had been part of my life from my earliest memories. I wasn't a super talented musician—I could play piano and guitar enough to get through some easy songs—but I couldn't imagine my life without music.

I was passionate about music history, music theory, and the importance of music and art in all aspects of education. I maybe wasn't an amazing singer or an accomplished musician, but I took my job at the center very seriously.

As head of the music department, I made sure our children were exposed to all manner of music and had the opportunities to learn different genres and styles, histories and theories, and were provided with not only the chance to listen to a variety of music, but also to learn how to read, write, and play music.

Many of the children we taught at the center—whether in our morning or afternoon school programs and classes, or in the after-school and summer programs and camps—would never become virtuosos, but I was damned proud of the fact they'd recognize how important music was in our lives.

We had data to back our services—large percentages of the kids who attended our Cravenwood Education Center had higher academic scores and lower instances of behavior problems.

Were we aware many other factors could be involved in those numbers? Sure, but there was no proof our program *wasn't* helpful, so we just went with it.

On my way to grab a drink at Cravin'-a-Cup, I let my mind wander to why I was so worked up over getting a new director—what had my stomach in crampy little knots.

Number one, I didn't do well with change.

I knew this and knew it well.

As a kid, I didn't understand it.

As an adult, I was self-aware enough to understand it and know where it came from—thanks to therapy, I definitely hadn't gotten to that point by myself.

My mom...well, she'd been gone for several years thanks to a drug overdose...but from the beginning, she was a pretty crap mom overall. After I was born—and I would always be grateful for the father Julian and I shared—she went off the deep end and never really got herself back to a stable point.

Just when I'd start to think maybe things were settling, she'd do something to rock my world and change things up. Honestly, the best thing she ever did was send me to live with my dad and Julian, but by that point, a lot of damage had been done.

Eight years of moving to a different crappy apartment every month. Eight years of never knowing if I'd have a bed, a couch, or a floor to sleep on. Constantly being the new kid in school, or having to answer questions when I came back to a former school. New men in and out of Mom's life.

Looking back, it wasn't hard to figure out how those first eight years had shaped my life. Music had been my only constant, even as a young kid.

So, yeah, I didn't like change and the new director was a change.

I also worried he'd want to change the music program I'd worked so hard to build. I'd put a lot into the program and I wasn't looking forward to him wanting to upend my hard work.

Two, I was low-key worried the new director wasn't going to like me.

The fear of people not liking me was as deep-seated as hating change.

Before Mom sent me to live with Dad and Julian, she brought guy after guy into the house. I remember wishing at least one of them would like Mom and me enough to stick around and build a family.

Mom's *dating* habits were likely why I flitted from guy to guy, never even considering settling—but maybe also why Bash had struck a chord deep within me. Maybe my psyche saw Bash as *the one* who would stick around.

Which was crazy because he'd already said his new job was temporary.

When I moved in with Dad and Julian at age eight, Julian was nineteen. I already knew there was something different about me and I worried they'd kick me out if they knew—hindsight is twenty-twenty because Dad is the most over-the-top supportive parent in the world—and I strived to never do or be anything they didn't like.

I remembered Julian having friends over and how badly I wanted them to like me. Getting laughs, being outlandishly upfront and saying whatever was on my mind, and making myself sound bigger and better than my actual sad reality were all defense mechanisms and ways to get people to like me.

In all actuality, being the kid who said whatever was on my mind in order to get some laughs was so damn ridiculous. If I'd *really* said what was on my mind, I would have broken down crying while begging those around me to just please like me.

So, yeah, I was definitely worried the new boss wouldn't like me.

Some pretty heavy therapy had helped me work through my past. I learned ways to cope with change and *trying* not to worry when people inevitably didn't like me, but it wasn't easy and it didn't happen quickly.

After a quick chat with Leighton while he made a large black coffee and my favorite butterfly pea flower tea, I filled a bag with cream and sugar and headed toward the center.

I had no clue if my new boss liked coffee, but I figured

it was a nice peace offering either way. If he preferred cream and sugar, I had that covered too.

I may have been worried about the change and the new guy not liking me, but I damned sure wasn't going to give up without a fight. I wasn't exactly sure what I was going to have to fight, but I was ready.

I'd turn on my Ollie charm and do whatever it took to show the man I was the best at what I did and the ed center would be lost without me.

I just needed to make a good impression on the first day.

My phone buzzed with a text.

From Bash.

Bash: *If you're still willing, I'd like information about the possible apartment.*

I COULDN'T HELP the huge smile on my face.

Me: *Sure thing. Let me talk to the apartment manager and I'll get back with you tonight if that's okay.*

Bash: *Sounds good. Thank you.*

Bash: *Have a good day, Oliver.*

. . .

I BIT MY LIP, not even attempting to hold back the giddy little laugh escaping me.

Me: You too, Sebastian.

MAYBE THIS DAY wasn't going to be so bad after all.

FOUR

Bash
_____

FUCK.

My.

Life.

I was a damned forty-two-year-old moron and I deserved the throbbing headache and queasy stomach from way too many drinks the night before my first day at a new job.

What the hell had I been thinking?

Clearly, nothing good.

I'd had every intent of going to the bar on Cravenwood Block and nursing a whiskey sour for an hour or so as I did some people watching and got a feel for my new, albeit temporary, home.

After making the mistake of downing drink number one, I'd ordered another meant for actual sipping. I wasn't driving home, but I knew my limits.

All thoughts of limits and plans had shot right out the proverbial window when I'd seen Ollie on the dance floor.

I'd watched him chat, laugh, and shake his ass through a couple drinks.

I should have left the moment I saw him make his way to the bar for another green drink—of course he was drinking something pretty—but I sat there like a fool.

And he saw me.

I couldn't have escaped if I wanted to.

At least I'd been smart enough to order one last drink and close my tab before I drank myself into oblivion just to keep Ollie by my side and talking.

But I hadn't stopped drinking in time and the morning was a rude reminder of all of my regrets from the night before. I hadn't gotten completely wasted, but I also wasn't twenty-one anymore and my body sure as hell wasn't letting me forget that fact.

Allowing the scalding hot water of my shower to pummel my forehead, I realized the number of drinks were really my *only* regret.

Talking and laughing with Ollie were the exact opposite of regret. Something about that man—I wanted to refer to him as a *kid*, but that wasn't accurate...he wasn't a child, just younger than me by several years—brought a levity and easiness to conversation I hadn't enjoyed in years.

I thought back to the blow job Ollie offered.

Did I regret not taking him up on that?

My dick did.

But I'd meant what I said about Ollie being worth more than five minutes on his knees in a bar bathroom.

How I knew that, I had no clue. But deep inside, I

knew with certainty Ollie was different and deserved the world.

Why couldn't I stop the niggling thought *I* should be the one to give him what he deserved?

What a mess my head was in.

I was attracted and drawn to a way-too-young man, starting a job I wasn't thrilled about, needing a place to live, and had LuLu to think about too.

The job was probably the easiest part.

The fact I wasn't going to be there long made it a bit harder, but also somewhat easier. I'd go in, change things for the better if needed, leave the place a touch above its current position, and maybe even learn something while I was at it.

The thought of temporary housing *with* the man I was attracted to was insane and exciting. I definitely needed my head examined.

LuLu was another thing altogether. The move to Cravenwood Block was *good* in that it put me closer, but I wasn't planning on sticking around.

The whole situation was simply a reset.

A chance to gather myself, recharge, and prepare for bigger and better.

Getting a place to live was the most important next step—outside of meeting my new staff. I wasn't even allowing myself to *think* about anything with Oliver until I was settled into a work routine and had a place to live.

Then I'd maybe consider asking him out.

Maybe.

He was so young.

I'd never gone for a younger man before.

In fact, *I'd* always been the younger man.

I chuckled humorlessly.

At forty-two, I wasn't ancient, but finding interested older men to date sometimes seemed like searching for a needle in a haystack.

Was I now the older guy?

Did I even want the entanglement of dating?

Especially dating a younger guy?

What could we possibly have in common?

My dick twitched as I turned off the shower.

Sex.

We'd likely have sex in common.

There was no time for getting off that morning—even if the thought of picturing a certain red head with dark brown eyes while I stroked one out had appeal.

Padding from the empty bathroom to the empty bedroom in a townhouse that wasn't mine anymore—had never been mine—I rummaged through my shaving kit for some aspirin and an Alka-Seltzer.

Breakfast of champions.

I'd toss a protein bar in my bag in case stopping for flowers took longer than I hoped and I wasn't able to grab coffee and a sandwich on the way to work.

I wanted to be there before everyone else.

After dressing in dark gray pants, a light gray shirt, dark gray fitted vest, and an eggplant colored tie, I ran some product through my hair in hopes of a purposely-messy-but-stylish look.

With my stomach still so-so and my head still pounding, I slipped on black dress shoes, packed my bag with all things pertinent to work, and headed out the door while ordering a ride.

A few moments later, I was in the back seat of an Uber heading toward Cravenwood Block. I took a moment to check on the flower shop's hours—thank god they were open early, I hadn't even given thought to them opening later in the morning. Maybe they got a lot of people like me who wanted to start the day with a cheerful bouquet while hoping to make a good impression.

Checking the time, I realized I'd likely be pushing it to get flowers *and* coffee.

Damn.

Flowers first.

Maybe I could run out for coffee once I'd met everyone.

In fact, maybe I could offer to do a coffee run as a nice gesture.

I couldn't say I was *worried* about my new team liking me, but it always made everything run more smoothly if working relationships were somewhat friendly—without crossing the line, of course.

Taking the next several moments to just breathe and hope to hell my head stopped throbbing, I gave myself a little pep talk about the day.

Once on Cravenwood Block, I thanked the driver and exited the car in front of Cravenwood Flowers just as the lady inside flipped the door sign to *open*.

Multitasking at my best—and hoping it wasn't *too* early for a text—I tapped out a message to Ollie as I headed into the flower shop.

. . .

Me: If you're still willing, I'd like information about the possible apartment.

"GOOD MORNING," the cheery employee said. "How can I help you?"

"Well, I'm starting a new job and I wanted to get flowers for my employees. I know for a fact I need seven bouquets and I want one for my own office. Would I be able to go with ten just in case there are people I'm forgetting? Being new there, I'm not one hundred percent sure on names and positions." My phone buzzed in my pocket, but I ignored it while speaking with...I checked her nametag...Maggie about the flowers.

"Sure thing. We have economy-price bouquets for seven dollars apiece. The next step up is ten dollars and those are very nice. If you want to go with the ten-dollar flowers, I can offer a bulk discount which makes them almost the same price as the economy ones, but you're getting more flowers for a better deal." Maggie pulled out a pad of paper and grabbed a pen.

"Let's do the ten-dollar ones and the discount sounds great. I want ones they can put on their desk or take home to display—just a goodwill gesture for the first day." I smiled. "I'll trust you on types and colors and all that."

"Perfect. I've got what you need already made up. If you'll give me five minutes, I'll get everything packaged and have you on your way."

"Sounds good. Thank you." I pulled out my phone to check the message.

. . .

Oliver: Sure thing. Let me talk to the apartment manager and I'll get back with you tonight if that's okay.

I WASN'T sure if my smile was because I heard from Oliver or because I maybe had the chance at an apartment.

Me: Sounds good. Thank you.

Me: Have a good day, Oliver.

I COULDN'T HELP the zing that traveled through me when I thought of teasing him. I could almost picture the look on his face.

Oliver: You too, Sebastian.

CHUCKLING, I tucked my phone in my pocket and browsed the flower shop until Maggie had my order ready. After paying, I headed down the block. Definitely no time for coffee, but my head and stomach were luckily settling themselves.

I was pretty sure I wouldn't be drinking again for a while.

Letting myself in the door nearest my office, I realized the building alarm was already disabled. Maybe another early-bird like myself? Or more likely a member of the cleaning crew.

I flipped on the lights in my part of the hallway and made my way to my office.

Glancing around for a place to put the huge package of flowers, I suddenly realized I hadn't even thought about vases.

Shit.

Complete oversight on my part.

I kept a vase in my classroom when I taught high school, and in my office when I taught college classes.

Grabbing a notepad, I started what I figured would be a long to-do list and reminders and items to purchase.

Where could I get ten vases?

Granted, with some wet paper towels wrapped around them, most of the flowers would be fine until the owners got them home and into water, but I'd really liked the idea of everyone having bright, colorful beauties on their desks.

Maybe the kitchen?

I'd try there first and then the art room.

Thirty minutes later—so much for being productive before our first day staff meeting—I'd successfully gathered ten pseudo vases from the kitchen and the art room.

Assuming *some* might have their own, I'd have the ones I found as a backup when I handed out the flowers.

Along with an apology to the kitchen staff and art team *and* an expectation that the containers be washed and returned within a week.

Was I being a hard nose? Providing flowers but also handing out stipulations?

Screw it. I'd bought everyone flowers.

If they needed a temporary vase, I'd give them one.

There was nothing wrong with expecting the containers be returned in a timely manner.

While I arranged things in the large group instruction room, my phone buzzed.

Oliver: Hey, I actually talked to the apartment manager this morning. He says the room in our place is yours if you want to give him a call and get things set up.

MY STOMACH FLIP-FLOPPED.

Me: Just like that?

Oliver: Well, he's my brother :) I kinda have an in. His name is Julian. 450-410-1977. He's an early riser and expecting your call.

WELL, hell. I certainly hadn't expected that.

I checked the time. Since I'd arrived early, I had about twenty minutes to spare—go get coffee or call Julian?

Feeling a bit giddy about the weight of finding a place to live being lifted from my shoulders, I punched the number into my phone.

"Julian Barrows, Cravenwood Apartment Manager," a friendly voice answered.

"Good morning. My name is Sebastian Evans. Oliver— um, *Ollie*—gave me your information regarding a room for rent in your complex?" Nerves suddenly flooded over me.

"Mornin', Mr. Evans—"

"Bash, please."

"Ollie's vouched for you, Bash. I don't usually work up the contract without an in-person meeting and tour of the place, but if you're in a hurry to get the process started, I can make an exception. My little brother indicated you were in a bind and needed the place sooner rather than later."

I didn't miss the insinuation in Julian's words. He was nice, friendly, and willing to help, but the emphasis on *little brother* left no room for misunderstanding, he wanted to be damn sure I understood he wouldn't stand for Ollie coming to any harm.

"That would be amazing." I cleared my throat. "One quick question, do you allow month-by-month rentals? Or a six-month contract? I don't know how long I'll be at this job and I'd rather not be locked into a year-long lease."

Julian paused. "Definitely not month-by-month and the last six-month lease turned into an issue. I can tell you, if you need out before the lease comes up for renewal, I've always got a waiting list of folks ready to take over a lease."

"There's a waiting list?"

Julian chuckled. "What can I say? I love my brother and *mostly* trust his judgment. If he says he knows someone who needs a room, I don't mind bumping a name to the top of the list."

"Well, I definitely appreciate that." I paused, thinking about being tied to a whole year here. It was a nice location, one of the best in Midtown. If Julian could easily get someone to take over my lease, I wouldn't be stuck. "Let's get started."

We discussed monthly rent—which ended up being a price there was no way I could refuse—and information Julian would need from me. He promised to email me forms that needed signatures as soon as we hung up and I assured him I'd send the needed documents by lunchtime —perks of having all my pertinent information in an online file *and* having a scanner at work.

"You want to come see the place? Move some things in?" Julian asked.

"Can I? Without final paperwork?"

Julian huffed out a chuckle. "You're employed. I can't imagine you taking the time and effort to make the call and send the information needed if you thought you'd be denied over credit or income or something similar. I'm assuming all will go well—and trusting both you and Ollie to make sure I don't regret the decision."

"Perfect. There's nothing surprising or damning in the information I'll be sending. I don't have much of anything to move in, but I'd like to see the place and get an idea of which items I can bring out of storage."

"I'll give some times I'm available in the email and we can set something up from there. Feel free to text me any questions."

I thanked him and hung up.

Ten minutes until the staff meeting I'd requested.

I'd need to skip the happy dance I wanted to do.

My hangover was forgotten.

I had a place to live.

With Ollie.

Damn.

I wasn't sure whether to be thrilled or filled with dread.

I'd have to think about that later.

Folks began arriving to the meeting and I turned on the charm.

"Good morning," I greeted, sticking out my hand to shake. "Sebastian Evans." *Bash* was reserved more for outside of work.

"Good morning, nice to meet you," a man in joggers and a hoodie said, returning my handshake. "Devonte Jones, health and wellness department."

"Hi, good to meet you," an older woman replied as she took my offered hand. "I'm Angela, I work the front office."

As more and more people arrived, I did my best to be friendly and welcoming, trying to make mental note of all the names and positions.

The Cravenwood Education Center had a full staff with teachers and assistants in the English Language Arts, STEM, Music, Art, and Health & Wellness departments, along with a kitchen staff and front office staff.

As the director, I was taking over more of a behind-the-scenes administration role while the head of each department acted as the top level in their department's chain of command. Behavior issues or any other concerns went to the department head first. If the issue couldn't be solved or needed more intervention, the department head would come to me.

According to the owner of the center—an elderly man who had indicated his daughter would soon be taking over —behaviors were seldom an issue, and the staff ran the place like a well-oiled machine.

From what I could gather in speaking with the owner, he didn't often involve himself with the day-to-day operations—although, he hinted his daughter would likely be a lot more hands-on—but the Cravenwood Education Center was top-notch and boasted of small-group instruction, tutoring, summer camps, after-school programs, and a low staff-to-student ratio.

"Do we have most of our team?" I asked. My stomach was back to churning—this time with nerves rather than alcohol—but I felt confident and ready to get the day started.

"Mayer isn't here yet," a young man with tattoos and piercings spoke up. "Probably stopped for his butterfly pea flower tea."

Everyone smiled fondly as if this Mayer was known to pick up a morning drink over being a couple minutes early to his staff meetings. A pang of jealousy zipped through me over the guy getting his drink when I hadn't had time for mine.

"Well, we still have a couple minutes. Feel free to chat and we'll start at the top of the hour." I would have rather started right then, but it wasn't truly fair to start before the actual time of the meeting, so I was willing to wait.

Perusing my notes, I made an effort to jog my memory of the main things I wanted to say.

At exactly the top of the hour, a man walked into the large group instruction room. "Sorry, I stopped for my tea."

The gathered staff chuckled as if they'd expected as much.

I turned to smile at the newcomer.

And almost fell over to see him standing with two drink cups and a brown paper bag in his hands.

Fuck.

My.

Life.

FIVE

Ollie

_____

OH.

My.

God.

Bash was my new director?

For a split second, my heart soared and I thought of all the ways this was going to be absolutely epic.

Then I crashed as I realized with horror I'd offered—several times—to suck off my new boss.

Fucking.

Hell.

For the first time in my life, I didn't have some sort of mouthy quip or funny comment to cover for my anxiety and unsureness.

This was fine.

Everything was fine.

He stood there in his dress pants that fit him like a damn glove, a button up, and a vest—who the hell could not only pull off a vest but make it look fucking sexy as hell? Apparently, Bash could. His straight brown hair was styled, but I could already see he'd shoved his hand through it, and his scruff-that-should-have-looked-unkempt beckoned me run my fingers through it.

Biting my lip, begging Bash with my eyes to please not fire me on the spot, I quickly made my way to the front of the room and handed him the coffee and bag.

"Sorry I'm late." I stepped backward, praying I'd make it to my seat without incident, but also thinking it would be best if the ground opened up and swallowed me whole. "Um, I brought coffee."

For a brief moment, Bash stared at me, unblinking. Then he cleared his throat, gave a nod, and held out the hand not holding a coffee cup. "Very much appreciated. Sebastian Evans. And you are?"

Huh?

Oh, right.

Probably best not to start with the whole center knowing I'd all but begged my new boss to shove his dick down my throat.

"Ollie Mayer," I said. "Music department head."

"Nice to meet you, Mr. Mayer. We're just getting started."

Properly dismissed, I clutched my butterfly pea flower tea and somehow made my way to an empty chair.

This was so not fine.

What the fuck was going on?

Was the universe conspiring against me?

If I hadn't offered to give him head, I wouldn't be in such a fiasco.

But as it was, I'd suggested oral sex to my boss, offered him a place to live—in a room he didn't realize he'd be sharing with me—and told him I was highly interested in dating him.

Taking a long sip of the tea, honestly wishing it was something a bit stronger even though the lingering headache from my current hangover wasn't a fan of that idea, and attempted to focus on what Bash—*Mr. Evans? Sebastian?* What the hell was I supposed to call him?—was saying.

He planned to keep things mostly the same for the time being, wanted the transition to be as smooth as possible, wanted us to know his door was always open, and he'd heard wonderful things about the center and its staff.

Blah.

Blah.

Blah.

Did he not realize this was a catastrophe?

Was he really just standing up there doing his best bossy-boss job and ignoring the fact one of his new employees propositioned him?

Do you think it would be better if he stopped the meeting to let everyone know the two of you know each other and how?

Fuck.

No.

Finally, the meeting wrapped up since the morning group of students would be coming in soon.

"I'm looking forward to my time here. As a first day gift, I've brought flowers for everyone's desk," Sebastian said, gesturing toward a counter top strewn with bouquets. "If you have your own vase, please feel free to use it." He smiled sheepishly. "I may not have thought things out very well and realized we might not all have vases on hand, so I borrowed some items that might work from the art room and kitchen—if you use any of those, please be sure they are returned as good as new and within a week." He smiled in what looked like relief as chuckles sounded around the room. "Please, take your pick of flowers, and have a great day."

As the entire room started shuffling and packing up, Sebastian cleared his throat and spoke over the low murmur of people starting their day. "I'd like to meet with each department head throughout today and tomorrow. Mr. Mayer, I'll start with you and work my way through the departments. The rest of you, please email me available times." He made direct eye contact with me and I wasn't sure whether I wanted to shiver at how damn sexy he looked or piss my pants because he looked so fucking serious.

I nodded and sipped my tea, hoping for fortification.

"My office. Now," Sebastian growled as he walked past me.

Glancing around to see if anyone else had heard him, I inwardly whimpered. No one seemed to be paying any attention as they fawned over the flowers. Sebastian looked and sounded as if he was going to kill me and no one would even realize I was gone until the next staff meeting. Or until some kid wet their pants during music circle and the teacher couldn't get ahold of the parent. Then they'd come looking for me and I'd be dead.

I grabbed my bag, clutched my tea tightly, and started to follow Sebastian to his office, but I paused and looked back toward the flowers.

Marching to the counter, I grabbed a bouquet and smiled at my colleagues. "Nice of him, huh?" I had my own vase in my office, so I skipped the loaners, and made my way toward my demise.

Popping my head into Sebastian's office, I gave what I hoped was a dazzling smile. "Thanks for the flowers, so sweet."

"Sit down." Sebastian pinched the bridge of his nose.

I sat, careful not to smoosh my flowers. "So," I laughed nervously, "this is slightly awkward."

"Did you know about this?"

"What?" My face scrunched in confusion. "Know about what?"

"Me working here," Sebastian bit out. "Were our little encounters all part of a game? See if you could trip me up, get me wrapped around your little finger before I even started the job?"

"I mean this as respectfully as one can, but fuck off, *Mr. Evans*." I stood and grabbed my belongings. "One, how would I have known some random hottie I saw in the diner was going to be my new boss—hell, I thought my new boss was going to be old and decrepit with dentures and a comb over. Two, get over your damn self. Three, just because some people in your past screwed you over doesn't mean everyone is out to get you." Hefting my bag and cradling my flowers, I took a sip of tea to calm the words raging to escape me. "I'm *really* sorry for offering to suck you off—not because I don't want to, but you know, because you're now my boss and, surprise, surprise, it's made things awkward—but I'd like to think, since neither of us could have seen this coming, you'll choose to not hold it against me."

Sebastian stood and moved closer, rubbing a hand over his forehead with a scowl. "I'm sorry," he sighed. "It's become a knee-jerk reaction to be suspicious. Obviously, neither of us knew we'd be working together. I need to apologize for even contemplating your offer. Please let Julian know how sorry I am about wasting his time."

"Wait, what? I get me begging to blow you was inappropriate—well, maybe not at the time, maybe just a bit too forward—and now that I know you're my boss, I clearly won't offer random oral sex unless we come to some sort of an agreement about personal and professional boundaries." I tossed my empty cup into his trashcan. "But turning down a kick-ass apartment with what I'm guessing is killer rent compared to what you've found in other less-amazing places to live is just dumb."

Sebastian ran a hand over his sexy scruff. "I'm your boss now. That fact means nothing is happening between us. It also means us living together seems to be tempting fate and overall not a good idea."

"I disagree."

"Of course you do," he sighed.

I took a bit of hope in the tiny crook of a smile teasing the corner of his lips.

"You're my boss *now*. You weren't my boss at the diner or the bar. You weren't my boss when we exchanged numbers. You weren't my boss when I told you I'd like to go out with you and very much meant every word." I shrugged. "I'm young, but I'm good at my job. Even though I may come off like I don't have two brain cells, I actually *am* intelligent and responsible enough to keep my personal life separate from my professional life. And if you give up the chance to live within a five-minute walk from work, in an amazing apartment with great people, and rent that would make others cry in envy, that's your own dumbass decision."

Sebastian huffed. "You really think we can live *and* work together without there being some sort of issue?" He sounded tired and defeated, but a tiny bit hopeful.

"Honestly, I don't know. I know I like you. I know I was very serious about maybe dating. I know you won't find a better apartment." I rolled my eyes. "And despite the fact I offered to get on my knees for you, I know I can completely control myself at work." I glanced down at the flowers, something catching in my throat. "I also know no one has ever bought me flowers. I know no one has ever told me I'm worth more than five minutes on my knees. I'm not suggesting we're looking at a happily ever after, but I'm willing to have fun with *now* if you can pull your head out of your ass long enough to realize us working together doesn't *have* to be a nail in the coffin of whatever potential there is between us."

Sebastian frowned. "I don't even know how to answer any of that."

"It's okay, I kinda took myself by surprise too. I started the morning thinking I was buying coffee for some old man who was going to fuck up my job. Then I realize it's you and I dragged my ass to your office thinking you were going to fire me, but instead you pissed me off. Everything else is kinda a blur now." I checked the wall clock. "Look, I've got work to do. Ball's in your court. Decide to be my boss and nothing else, I'll continue doing the best I can at a job I love. Opt into the apartment and we're roommates only, I'll continue doing the best I can at a job I love. Decide to give us dating a try, I'll continue doing the best I can at a job I love. None of your options will stop me from doing my best and loving my job. Roommates? Dating? Those things don't affect *here*." I gestured around the office space.

"You're being very mature about all of this, Oliver," Sebastian said, that rough-edged voice like a soft caress to my balls.

I shrugged. "I can be mature when I want to be."

"And if things crash and burn? Where does that leave us? Roommates and working together with a ball of drama because dating didn't work out?"

I hefted my bag. "I guess it's a chance. But you're not even going to be around that long, right? Maybe we have fun while we can. As long as you don't turn into some serial killer or try to shut down my music department, I think we're grown enough to deal with a breakup if it gets to that point."

Sebastian sighed. "I'm just not sure it's a good idea."

At that point, I wasn't sure what *it* he was talking about, so I shrugged. "Your call. But don't be stupid."

He huffed. "Have a good day, Mr. Mayer."

My stomach dropped. His words sounded like a goodbye before we'd really even gotten a chance to say hello. I nodded. "You too, Mr. Evans."

I somehow got through my day without screaming—hopeful anticipation and resigned disappointment had me on the edge—but running a couple small groups, meeting with my teachers, and speaking to a couple parents made the day go by fairly quickly.

By the time I made my way to Cravin'-a-Cup, I wasn't sure what decision I hoped Sebastian made. On one hand, if he opted to find someplace else to live and speak to me only in boss capacity, I'd probably save myself a lot of heartache in the long run—even if my damn homo heart had already gone and gotten itself attached and hopeful.

On the other hand, if Sebastian opted to move in and be roommates only—no dating or extracurricular bedroom activities—I'd be dealing with frustrated pining for an entire year.

On the *other* other hand, if he moved in and gave into my good-natured charm and underrated sexual allure, we'd have to find a happy-medium between home and work. *Plus*, I'd likely still be heading toward heartache because he'd made it clear he wasn't sticking around.

"Damn, girl, rough day?" Leighton asked as he slid into the chair across from me. "I've got fifteen minutes. You want a drink? Snack? You can tell me all your troubles."

"Chai latte, extra shots, almond milk, iced. Please."

Leighton huffed. "As if I don't know how my bestie likes his afterschool drink. Scone? Cinnamon roll? Sandwich?"

"Turkey sandwich and a cookie, please." I handed him my card knowing he'd take care of everything and return to me with sustenance and a listening ear.

Leighton sometimes came off flaky, but he was one of the most genuine, caring, sunshiny people I'd ever met. He'd been hurt in the past, and I worried what this new *whatever* between him and Jett might bring, but he was fierce and strong. Whoever caught his eye and earned his love was definitely in for something special.

"Here ya go, baby doll." Leighton handed me my card —and no receipt, which likely meant he'd comped my order—along with my drink and food. "Now, tell me what ails you."

"I offered to give my boss a blow job," I muttered.

Leighton nearly spit out his drink. Once he'd swallowed and wiped his mouth, he gawked at me. "I'm sorry, *what*?"

"I offered my boss a blow job," I repeated.

"The old guy? With the comb over?"

I huffed. "Turns out, he's not old. Remember the guy from the diner? The funky, wise owl guy?"

Leighton's eyes nearly popped out of his head. "That's your new boss? Oh my god, you tried to suck him off at the diner *and* the bar, right?"

I didn't keep many secrets from Leighton.

I nodded miserably. "Yep. Then walked into the staff meeting this morning only to realize he's now my boss."

"And he fired you?" Leighton wrinkled his nose sympathetically.

"Oddly enough, no. I mean, I didn't proposition him *knowing* he was my boss, so he likely wouldn't have had much to go on."

"Ohhhhhh, wait, is he still going to move in?" Leighton propped his chin on his hand, completely invested in the story like any best friend should be.

"I don't know. I told him we could make it work and it

would be stupid if he gave up the apartment, but I really don't even know how I want it all to play out."

Leighton pursed his lips and checked his phone. "Sugar, I wish I could stay and chat, but my fifteen minutes are up. Jett and I have plans later, but we can talk more when I get home, okay? Everything will work out eventually."

I nodded, Leighton was ever the optimist. "Yeah, thanks for listening. I'll see you at home."

SIX

Bash

I STAYED in a nearby hotel my first few nights on Cravenwood Block. I called every single apartment within a feasible walking distance, and even gave in and called the ones a bit further out—I'd figure out transportation if I needed to—but there were no openings whatsoever. The *one* room I could have possibly had a chance with—if *four* other people turned it down first—was over double the monthly rent as the apartment with Ollie and Julian.

A few days into my new job, my head throbbing and my stomach churning at the potential disaster, I called Ollie into my office after the morning group arrived and classes started.

He walked in, looking pensive and damn good enough to eat—fucking *hell*, that was exactly why I needed to stay far, far away from Ollie Mayer, but damn if I didn't have to admit defeat.

"Yeah?" he said tentatively after sitting down and clearing his throat.

"If the offer still stands," I started, "I'd like the apartment."

A smiled spread across his face and I had stupid notions of wanting to make him smile like that all the time.

Fucking.

Hell.

This was going to be a long year.

Maybe six months should be my goal.

But LuLu had been excited to know I was going to be nearby.

The least I could do was commit to a year.

I held up a hand. "I'm not worried about the boss/employee status, but I do want to make it clear we're colleagues and roommates, nothing more." I absolutely had to keep telling myself that.

Ollie's face fell, but he nodded. "Gotcha."

"Can I start moving in after school today?"

"Yeah, that works." Ollie stood up and made his way to the door, paused and turned back to face me. "I gotta let you know, I stand by what I said. Nothing will stop me from doing my job. You may not want to explore anything between us—and I can take no for an answer—but I'm still interested, I can't just shut that off. Maybe living together will change my mind and I'll move on to the next hot guy, but I just want you to know the option is still available. For now." He gave a nod and walked out, shutting the door behind him.

Damn it.

That kid.

Kid.

I needed to remember that.

I'd never gone for a younger guy—or not *that* much younger. I'd always been attracted to older men. That was my type.

Right?

Caleb hadn't been an attraction, he'd been a momentary lack of judgement and a lot of regret.

Ollie wasn't my type.

I didn't go for his type of over-the-top innuendo or dogged determination.

Red hair hadn't done it for me in the past.

Blue eyes usually ticked my boxes, not a deep enough brown they made you feel like you couldn't even come up for air.

He was too young, too opposite of me, too much an employee, and definitely needed to be off-limits.

I'd told myself the only way I could share an apartment with him was if I drew a line in the sand and we both kept to our own sides.

I didn't mind casual friends. Hell, living with someone required respect and at least basic friendliness.

But nothing more.

Pushing the thought of Ollie's perfect ass in those jeans, his ludicrous offer to suck me off, and the niggling desire to figure out how to make him smile multiple times a day out of my head, I settled into long hours of paperwork, phone calls, meetings, and observing my new staff while I got to know the students and parents.

When the center finally shut its doors for the day, I was grateful I only had a short walk to the apartment. I'd retrieved my old camping sleeping bag from the storage facility and hoped I could at least crash on the floor of my new room if Julian confirmed the paperwork was taken care of.

I'd rent a truck again and get my bed and whatever else might fit moved in, hopefully sooner rather than later. It stung slightly to be working at a job I was over-qualified for and moving into an apartment with up to seven other people—like I was back in college living in a dorm or frat house—but I kept reminding myself I only needed to make it through a year. Then I could find a better job, get a house, and move on with my life—this was just a bump in the road.

I needed to be grateful I was closer to LuLu, I at least *had* a job—it would look good on a resume in addition to my other prior employment—and I had a place to live. Julian had been kind and helpful. Ollie—while definitely a bit much—was intelligent, successful, and friendly. Surely, they would opt to live with others who were much like them—I was hoping my new roommates weren't a bunch of wild party people. I could handle living with others, I just wasn't sure I could deal with stereotypical frat-boy behavior at my age.

"Bash," a voice called out behind me as I neared the apartment building.

I knew that voice.

Already.

I hated how I already knew that voice.

Wanted to see the smile that went with the words.

Fuck.

I had enough going on in my life. I didn't need my

damn head getting messed up with thoughts of a music department head with no filter.

He was too young.

He was my employee.

And he wasn't my type.

No matter that smile.

No matter that ass.

No matter how he smelled of strawberry mint.

He was a bad decision waiting to happen.

A distraction I didn't need, even in the short amount of time I'd be on Cravenwood Block.

I turned around to see Ollie rushing toward me, two icy drinks in hand.

I maybe didn't need the distraction or temptation to make a bad decision, but I *did* need a roommate to show me the apartment, so it wasn't like I could ignore the guy.

"I got you an iced coffee. Leighton gave me my chai latte for free, so I got this one for you and tipped him double." Ollie smiled as he handed over the drink.

"Thanks. Leighton?"

"One of our roommates and probably my closest friend aside from Julian—he works at Cravin'-a-Cup. Then there's Dean—he's best friends with Lucas who is a bartender at the Tap. Shaw works with Dean at the health center." Ollie nudged my arm as we walked into the lobby. "No worries, you'll get to know everyone quickly—they're all good people. Leighton's been rooming with Julian and me the longest. Jett, Shaw, Dean, and Lucas have all moved in just recently, but we all get along really well so far."

We reached the third floor and Ollie walked me to the farthest door down the hallway.

"Corner apartment is the best, and you'll love the rooftop access." He unlocked the door and ushered me inside.

I had to admit I was impressed with the place.

Spacious.

Contemporary yet homey.

And extremely clean.

I don't know why, but I guess I'd been expecting dust, stains on the carpet, moldy food, and an unknown stench.

But the living room was bright and airy, no mess in sight, and a faint scent of citrus floated on the air.

"This is nice," I said.

"You look surprised." Ollie cocked his head. "Were you expecting something from a really bad college dorm gay gang bang porn clip?"

I closed my eyes.

There was the no filter.

Ollie laughed. "Sorry, but you need to get used to the fact I don't hold back. And I like to laugh. I won't laugh at the expense of others, but I'll definitely tell a story if it means getting some chuckles." He shook his head. "And the look on your face just now was priceless. Come on, professor, don't tell me you haven't enjoyed a good gang bang porn."

"Can I see the room?" I asked, choosing to ignore the comment—and the damn images Ollie's words set to motion in my mind.

Julian had texted earlier to let me know the paperwork had been finalized and I was welcome to move in—I had a feeling Ollie had been behind that message. I'd already paid the deposit. First month's rent was set to come out soon. Everything had fallen into place easily.

Almost too easily.

"Sure." Ollie pointed to an orange door. "That one is Julian and Shaw. The green one is Dean and Lucas."

As my damn head caught up with his words and calculated numbers, my stomach sank.

Holy.

Fucking.

Shit.

"The purple one is Leighton and Jett." He pointed to the blue door. "And *this* is where the Ollie magic takes place."

"We share a room?" I bit out, pinching the bridge of my nose.

Ollie blinked.

"Well, obviously. Mine was the only one left, so it's one of those *you get what you get and don't throw a fit* type situations." He shrugged. "No worries, my bed is plenty big enough for two. I usually only get cuddly on cold nights. I'll keep my clothes on for the first week or so as you settle in. Promise I won't straddle you and go for a ride—at least, not without permission," he said with a wink.

There was no way this was happening.

There was also no way I could share a room with Ollie.

Let alone share a damn *bed*.

Shit.

I should have asked *a lot* more questions.

Should have been smart enough to see the place *before* paying the deposit.

But for real, *how* was the information not readily shared? Shouldn't the buyer have been made aware?

Fuck.

Would Julian give me my deposit back?

I could probably stop payment on the rent.

It maybe would take a bit of arguing, but I could probably get out of the lease. Julian hadn't said I was *sharing* a room—truly, failure to disclose was an out, right?

Why was my head almost as caught up in the thought of sharing a bed with Ollie and gripping his hips as he rode me as it should have been in figuring out a way to *not* share a room—*and a bed*—with him?

Fuck.

Ollie burst out laughing. "Damn, man, for someone as smart and successful as you, you sure are gullible." He pushed open the blue door. "This is our room, but it has two very separate bedrooms. Don't get me wrong, my bed is open and available for any and all cuddling and riding you might want to do, but from the look of sheer terror on your face, I'm guessing we're not to that point yet."

He stepped close and patted my cheek.

"Breathe, Bash. It's all good. We share a bathroom with Lucas and Dean, and this little foyer slash lounge area is ours, but the bedrooms are separate. You even get a door with a lock to keep horny little Ollies out."

His hand lingered a split second too long on my skin, the warm zing between our bodies making me want to turn my head and press a kiss into his palm. We stood for a moment longer than necessary before I finally broke from the trance he'd put me in, glancing toward the bedroom door.

"This one is yours." Ollie pointed, an airy chuckle escaping him as he opened the door. "Definitely room for a bed and dresser, I think a desk is doable too. The closet isn't *great*, but it's decent."

Between the completely unwanted, unexpected, and inappropriate thoughts I was having about Ollie and the whiplash my mind and emotions had been through in the last few days—hell, pretty much ever since I caught Randal with the pool boy...god, how cliché—I wasn't sure I could make a sound decision at that moment if my life depended on it.

"Can I..." I paused to clear my throat. "Can I have a moment?"

Ollie cocked his head, studying me with curiosity and what appeared to be understanding. "Sure thing. Take all the time you need. Pretty sure Julian and I could help move your furniture this evening if you'd like to get that taken care of, but no pressure." He gestured toward the door. "I'll be in the kitchen."

He mercifully closed the door behind him and I took a deep breath as I studied the room. It was nice. Hardwood floor, neutral paint scheme, a fairly decent view of Cravenwood, and a closet that was actually larger than the one I'd had at the townhouse.

My bed and dresser would definitely fit, and I was pretty sure my desk would as well. Maybe I'd do bed and dresser first and see if I even wanted the desk later. I'd been bringing work home for much too long, perhaps now was the time to break that habit. Work at work, rest and rejuvenate at home.

Traitorous thoughts immediately shot to Ollie and how fun it might be to rejuvenate in the evenings and on weekends with him.

Fuck.

I really didn't see an option other than taking the room. There weren't any others close by, the rent was amazing, it was a five-minute walk to work, and I'd already started payment.

I was forty-two years old, for fuck's sake, I could ignore an attraction to a man who was much too young for me. Even if that attraction went beyond the physical and had begun to haunt my every waking thought, I would *not* be pigeonholed into the stereotypical midlife crisis by getting involved with a man half my age.

Dating and sex wasn't something I *needed* at that point in my life.

I'd had my fun way back in my younger days.

I'd done the whole pseudo-serious relationship with Randal.

I'd done the whole sordid breakup.

Hell, I even had the slanderous scandal in my past—as wildly fabricated as it was.

With over two decades of teaching both high school English and college level intro to teaching classes under my belt, the position at the education center was a nice change of pace—even if it felt like a demotion of sorts. I'd take it as a chance to reset and add variety to my resume.

The new job and location would give me a fresh perspective until I could find something better.

I'd enjoy my extra time with LuLu until I was able to move on.

Once I was in a location and job where I was *truly* meant to be, I could consider if and when I wanted to start dating again. Honestly, at this point, dating and sex felt more like a chore than something to be enjoyed.

Good luck, asshole. If that whole little self-talk speech of yours is what you're holding onto in hopes of staying away from Ollie and not getting sucked into this place, you're in for quite the disappointment.

I rolled my eyes at the niggling thoughts in the back of my head.

I didn't need *luck* to avoid Ollie and I certainly wasn't at risk of getting sucked into this place.

I had a year or less to leave the education center better than I found it, spend time with LuLu, maybe make some friends, and expand my work history for the better job just around the corner.

Ollie had no bearing other than being a friendly roommate and efficient employee.

Cravenwood Block meant nothing to me other than being a decent place to live.

The men I would be living with were strangers at this point and likely would end up being enjoyable acquaintances, perhaps friends.

I wasn't the type to get emotionally involved in people or places—with the exception of LuLu.

I gave a final glance out the window and a quick nod of affirmation.

I could make this work.

Feeling good about my decision, I headed to the kitchen to find Ollie.

If Julian and his little brother could help me move furniture in sooner rather than later, I'd be set to get this next stretch of time started and over with, ready to journey toward the *better* in my life.

This was just a bump in the road.

Just as I walked into the kitchen, I heard Ollie swear and something clatter. Glancing toward the sink where Ollie stood, I watched in horrified fascination as he stripped his shirt over his head.

His skin was paler than mine, but had a warm hue. Broad shoulders, a narrow waist, two dimples just above his ass—visible only because his damn jeans rode low on his hips, the barest hint of black underwear peeking above the waistband.

Ollie turned and yelped. "Shit, sorry. Spilled milk on me, I'm a klutz." He held his wadded up, soiled shirt in his hand. "Just gonna put this in the laundry."

As pretty as his back had been, Ollie's front had no trouble measuring up. A smattering of chest hair the same shade as the dark red on his head—no, I wouldn't allow myself to wonder if the same color I glimpsed trailing over his pale stomach and under his jeans continued to other places. He wasn't buff and cut, but he had light definition in his chest and abs, along with the shadow of a V seeming to scream *look here, you old perv* as I tried to put my eyes anywhere but on his body.

"No use crying over spilled milk," I muttered.

Ollie winked and walked around me, leaving the scent

of strawberry mint in his wake. Was it his shampoo? Gum? Hair product?

Fuck.

I didn't need to think about how Ollie smelled.

It didn't matter why he smelled like strawberry mint.

It didn't matter I suddenly wanted to bury my face in him and breathe deeply, nipping and sucking at those coppery nipples, swirling my tongue around his navel.

"Good thing," a voice behind me announced. "Ollie drinks chocolate milk like it's going out of style and somehow figures out a way to spill it almost every single time."

A stunningly gorgeous man with blond hair and breathtaking gray eyes smiled at me, a silver earring sparkling in his ear as he pushed a chunk of hair from his face.

"Hi, I'm Leighton. You must be the new boss Ollie offered to blow. Are you going to move in? It's pretty nice here. Has he shown you the rooftop yet?"

I stood, speechless.

So, this was the best friend. Clearly having no filter was a similarity they shared. Was that just a thing with younger people these days? Saying whatever was on their mind, no thought to those around them?

And dear lord, when had I become such a curmudgeon?

"Oh my god," Ollie groused as he returned—sadly with a new shirt on, but it was truly for the best if my damn head was going to get itself screwed on correctly. "Can we not bring that up, it's embarrassing." He glanced my way. "Unless you're reconsidering, because I'm totally still offering."

"Drink your chocolate milk," Leighton suggested. "I'm going to show my new roomie the rooftop. We'll be back."

Ollie looked as if he wanted to protest, but Leighton shot him a look, effectively shutting him up. Instead, he asked, "Want me to see if Julian can help move your stuff in tonight?"

"If it's not too much of an inconvenience. I can sleep on the floor for a while, I brought a sleeping bag."

"Nah, we'll get you moved in. Bring sheets and towels if you've got them. If not, we could go shopping."

I nodded, completely overwhelmed by Ollie, the number of things I needed to do, and the little burst of sunshine yanking me out the door for a rooftop tour.

"One of the perks to living on the top floor of Cravenwood Towers—aside from having great roommates like us—is the rooftop access." I followed Leighton up the stairs as he babbled. "Side note, don't ask why the apartment buildings are called *towers* when they're only like three stories tall—there's no good answer and it will just make you frustrated as you mull it over day after day. Anyway, living on the top floor means we get private access to the pool, dining area, sauna and jacuzzi, gym, and lounge area." He swiped his key card and pushed open the door. "See? It's great."

I stepped through the door and gave a low whistle. "Very nice." The whole rooftop was decorated with tiny, sparkly lights. The unlit tiki torches would add a nice ambience on a summer evening. The scent of chlorine from the pool and jacuzzi wafted on the air, reminding me of summer days growing up, swimming in my aunt's pool as I did everything possible to avoid my parents. "The sauna and gym alone would be worth the rent," I said, thinking of how nice it would be to come home to a workout and relaxing in the steamy heat.

"Yeah, we've got it good. We have small parties up here a lot—okay, that's not exactly true. Julian, Ollie, and I come up here a lot, but I'd like to think the eight of us will soon be having all sorts of fun up here." Leighton shrugged. "It's a great space with pretty much anything a person could want for rest and relaxation. I think the Cravenwood gym doesn't *love* that we get this access because it means several of us don't buy memberships over there, but who can blame us? I mean, you can probably tell I'm not a gym rat, so a membership would be wasted on me, but I have every intention of getting Jett up here to use the equipment so I can drool over him as he works out."

"Jett is…" I trailed off, waiting for Leighton's answer.

"My cupcake, my sugar lips, my world," he answered with a dreamy grin. "He might not be completely on board with the plan just yet, but we're getting there. He owns Cravin' Ink Designs." Leighton glanced around. "You know, this space truly is kinda the perfect porn setting. I can picture many a scene going down, especially in the gym area or sauna. I'm going to need to get Jett up here stat."

His words should have made me laugh and roll my eyes at the ridiculous notion. Instead, I found myself thinking of Ollie in a pair of skimpy trunks, dripping water as he hoisted himself from the pool, gleaming in the sun as he made his way to the sauna, throwing a sultry glance my way as he disappeared behind the door.

And oh, the scene that would await me if I followed him.

Shit.

For someone who'd just convinced himself he didn't really want or need the chore of dating or sex, I sure had nothing *but* on my mind.

Pulling myself from the sexy images Leighton had instigated, I walked to the railed edge to glance over, Cravenwood Block stretched out before me.

"Ollie will be a really good roommate," Leighton said from beside me, his words soft as if indicating he had shifted from fun tour guide to serious friend. "He's a really good person."

"Good to know."

"Maybe I should let you get to know him on your own, but I get the feeling you're one of those who thinks you can skim through life barely breaking the surface of anything serious. Or maybe you've been there, done that, and now want nothing to do with it, but that's whatever." Leighton leaned his arms on the railing. "Ollie talks a big game. He'll say whatever's on his mind. He's always down for getting a laugh. But he's got a past. He's got things on his mind he'll likely never say because they definitely won't get a laugh. I don't know exact details, but I know he wasn't in a good place when he went to live with Julian and his dad." He paused for a moment, gazing out over the town. "He loves what he does at the center. He's good with the kids and parents—he works hard and is dedicated to making sure his students learn the value of music. He's loyal and caring, and he deserves the best."

I cocked my head, studying Leighton. "And you think I'm not the best? This is you warning me away from him? I can assure you, I have no plans on getting involved with Oliver."

Leighton narrowed his eyes. "*Ollie* deserves the best and I have this weird feeling the two of you would be really good for each other. Maybe it's the way you appear to balance each other. I hear the words you're saying, but I've also seen the way you watch him. Just don't hurt him." He bit his lip. "And keep in mind things aren't always what they seem. Remember, Ollie talks a big game, but sometimes that's more a coverup than anything."

I suddenly wanted to wrap Ollie in my arms and kiss him until he told me everything about his past—I wanted to take away the hurt and know every single thing there was to know about him.

But that was dumb.

I wasn't even going to be around for long.

Ollie deserved someone who could stick around and make a life with him.

That someone wasn't me.

No matter how badly my stupid heart and mind had quickly and traitorously decided they wanted to be involved with him on every single level.

The kid and I could be friends.

Period.

Or we could keep it even less complicated and be colleagues only.

Sure, living in close proximity would bring a challenge, but it wasn't impossible.

By unspoken agreement, Leighton and I made our way back to the apartment.

Ollie glanced between us as if suspicious, but Leighton just gave him a hug and said goodbye on his way to meet Jett.

"Did he get weird?" Ollie asked. "He's amazing, but sometimes he gets weird. Like super protective. I'm protective of him too, but it's a strange combination of touched and annoyed when he does it to me."

"Nah, it was fine. Just showed me the rooftop. It's nice up there."

"Definitely. We're going to have a nacho party where we spread the chips out in a big line and pour all the toppings on and we just stand around drinking and eating nachos—almost like a trough, but we'll be civilized and use our hands." Ollie glanced down at his phone. "Cool. Julian can help move your stuff. He's got the apartment truck. You ready to go?"

I shrugged, checking to make sure I had my wallet and phone. "Yeah, I'm good."

Five minutes later, we were street-level climbing into Julian's truck.

I told him where the storage facility was located and he nodded.

During the ride, we made small talk about Julian's job, the education center, and the other roommates.

"Shaw is the sweetest thing," Ollie said, and I didn't miss the way Julian's knuckles whitened as he gripped the steering wheel. "I think he's got a lot of baggage from his past, sometimes he seems scared of his own shadow. But Dean says he's super at his job at the health center. Definitely want to get to know him better," he babbled on. "Dean is a doctor, but it's at the health center so I don't know that he's making a shit-ton of money. Lucas is like his best friend—I'll let you in on a secret, I think maybe Dean and Lucas are the only ones who don't realize they're madly in love and I've only known them for like two minutes—but anyway, Lucas is a bartender on the block. You met Leighton. His roommate is his newest crush—although, I think Jett may be falling for Leighton."

Julian shook his head. "I swear we aren't some big LGBTQ+ soap opera, my little brother just likes to tell everyone's business and create love stories in his head even when they might not actually exist."

"It's okay," I said. While I didn't usually get into gossip and hearsay, I didn't mind learning a bit about my new roommates. Plus, nothing being said was harmful or hateful.

Ollie turned the conversation back to the education center and we chatted about his colleagues and the positives of the place. "Honestly," he said as we neared the storage facility, "there's not a lot bad about it. The director before you was very well liked. She upset some people when budgets were cut, but we all adjusted to cover the cuts."

I frowned. "I wasn't told of budget cuts. The owner said the budget was sound and I'd actually have some wiggle room to make the changes I thought were best."

Ollie shrugged. "Weird. Maybe the former director's cuts put the center in a better financial position. I don't know; I liked Elise because she left me alone and let me do my job the way I saw fit."

I didn't miss Ollie's unsubtle hint, but I was more concerned about his budget comment. I didn't like knowing I was taking over a business with a questionable financial situation, but if what Ollie said was true, I definitely wanted to look into the books a bit and see just what was cut and why. I wasn't going to have my name attached to a place with financial issues.

By the time we got my bed and dresser, a large amount of clothing, and some personal affects loaded, I was hungry and ready to get the day over with.

"We'll get this carried up and then I'm going to the diner to eat, you wanna come with? I'll probably run to the grocery store too, need to get a few things." Ollie pretty much hadn't stopped talking the whole time we were together. In the past, that habit would have annoyed the shit out of me with most people, but I found I didn't mind it too much with him.

With Ollie it was almost endearing—even somewhat comforting—and wasn't that just a dollop of confusing and unwanted on top of everything else.

I helped Julian heft the dresser onto the dolly. "Food, yes." I wasn't sure why going to eat with Ollie seemed like a good idea—in reality, it was likely a terrible decision— but the words were out before I could stop them. "And I definitely need groceries. What's the procedure with food and supplies in the apartment?"

Ollie launched in a rundown of sharing food, buying groceries, and keeping certain items for strictly our own use. As we finished getting my furniture into my new room, he wrapped it up. "It works pretty well. We had a couple roommates before the five of you and never really had any trouble. As long as everyone is respectful, we'll be fine."

"You wanna put this bed together now?" Julian asked, his eyes drifting to Shaw as he spoke to me.

The younger man was gorgeous, but definitely seemed shy. I had a hard time picturing him working at the front desk of the health center, but Ollie indicated—despite being pretty much as new as me in the apartment and at his job—he had a great reputation as being a hard worker and valued member of the team.

Did Julian realize his eyes lit on fire whenever he looked at Shaw?

Was I the only one who recognized the look of longing Shaw returned?

Huh.

Maybe I was just letting Ollie's stories get to me.

"Nah, I'll just sleep on the mattress on the floor until I get time to put the frame together," I told Julian.

"Okay. There's a tool box under the sink, should have anything you'd need. If you find out there's something more you need, let me know and I can bring it home," Julian said.

"You wanna go eat with us?" Ollie asked.

Julian glanced at where Shaw was making toast and a bowl of cereal. "No thanks, I'm good."

I didn't miss the shy smile Shaw shot Julian's way.

"Okay, we'll be back later." Ollie grabbed my arm and led me toward the door. "Diner, groceries, and then bed. I'm exhausted and work is going to come early. Seems I have this new boss who is a total bear and expects on-time arrival and deadlines met."

I snorted. "Sounds ghastly."

"Right?" Ollie grinned up at me.

Shit.

I was in so much trouble.

———

Conversation with Ollie was easy.

Strangely easy.

Comfortable chit-chat had never been a thing for me—not with fellow teachers at the high school, not with colleagues at the college, not even with Randal when we were together—but with Ollie the words just flowed.

Of course, Ollie kept the conversation going and I just supplied answers mostly, but it was a noticeable difference compared to my past.

"So, we pretty much just take turns," Ollie explained as we walked toward the diner. "There's no set schedule, but we pitch in with chores and cooking as needed. A lot of times, schedules don't match up, so we're just on our own with meals. A good rule of thumb is *if you see it needs cleaned, clean it*. Do our own laundry—unless we have a set-up with someone to double up loads. Obviously, our own rooms are our responsibility. We share cleaning the bathroom with Lucas and Dean. The little foyer area of our room is our job. Living room, kitchen, all that is a shared effort. Mainly, in the kitchen, you make a mess, you clean the mess. Sometimes, we get into a routine of certain people making certain meals on specific days. Taco

Tuesdays, old fashioned Sunday dinners, that type thing, but it doesn't happen often—mainly just due to schedules being messed up."

Once we were seated, I said, "I'm usually not around on Wednesday evenings or Sunday afternoons."

Ollie cocked his head. "Church stuff?"

I raised a brow. "Do I strike you as a Bible thumper?"

He chuckled. "Not really, I just remember my mom dating some guy who went to church on Wednesdays and Sundays—beat the shit out of her on every day in between."

Wincing, and not liking the painful memories evident on Ollie's face, I shook my head. "Not church. I'm not a fan of organized religion for the most part. I just have... um, standing plans on those days."

Ollie shrugged as if not bothered by my secretive answer.

We placed our orders and continued to chat.

"Can I ask you something?" Ollie asked when our food arrived.

I studied him for a moment; he didn't *look* as if something outlandish was going to leave those soft pink lips. Nodding, I prepared myself for the unknown.

"Did you want the job at the center? Like, how did you get it?"

Cocking my head, I thought about his questions. "Why?"

He shrugged. "It seems like you're not really happy to be there. If I'm being honest, it kinda feels like you think you're better than the center and would rather be somewhere *worthy* of you."

My gut reaction was to lie and assure him that wasn't the case, but something told me to save my breath. Ollie had already read me and he deserved more than empty excuses.

Clearing my throat, I wiped a napkin over my mouth. "You're not completely wrong, but you're also not completely right."

Ollie waited patiently while dipping a fry in ranch, his eyes never leaving mine.

Feeling like a bug under a magnifying glass, I took a long sip of unsweetened tea. "I didn't actively seek out the job, that's true."

"And you feel like you're too good for it?" Ollie pressed.

"In some ways, yes."

Ollie raised his brows.

"Maybe not so much *too good*, more like overqualified? Or not the right kind of qualified? I've taught over twenty years in high school and college. I was one of the most requested instructors for first-year teacher preparation courses. I'm used to being a teacher, not a boss. My experience is managing a classroom, not in managing a business." I drummed my fingers on the table. "So, it's not so much I feel too good for the job, I just don't know that I'm the best fit. I'm not sure what I bring to the position is what's most needed."

"So, you're truly just here to ride it out before moving on to something bigger and better?" There was a slight edge to Ollie's words.

"Somewhat. The experience will add to my employability. I don't think I'm a negative fit for the job, just don't think I'm the perfect fit. I have no plans to make huge changes. I figure I'll add my own touch to the center, maybe leave it slightly better than I found it—not that I think there's anything terrible with it—and then move on to something different."

"Do you want to go back into the classroom?"

I shrugged. "Maybe? I can't say I miss the classroom as much as I thought I would. Teaching is often thankless and exhausting."

"Would you rather go back to high school or college? If you did go back?"

I pursed my lips. "Probably college. I love that age, but college gives me a lot more freedom. Dealing with adults is different than teens."

"What would you do if you didn't go back to the classroom?"

Shaking my head, I took a final bite of my meal. "Honestly, I don't know. Consultant? Administration?"

"How's that much different than running an education center?"

I raised a brow. "I guess I don't know that it is. You all seem to have a really good thing going on there. I'm not sure how much I'm needed."

"What if you give it a chance and find out you love it as much as most of us do?"

I smiled. "I'm not against that. I love the location. I love the purpose of the center. I just worry I'm not going to be challenged."

"But you're open to seeing how it plays out? Maybe you'll realize it's better than you thought?"

I nodded. "Sure, I'm willing to have an open mind."

Ollie grinned. "Well then, I'm set on making sure you see just how great the place is. We do a lot of good." He cocked his head and studied me. "And I'd like to think maybe you weren't looking for the center, but in the long run, you'll figure out it's exactly what you needed. I think, once you loosen up and get to know people, you'll realize what an all-around perfect fit this whole place is for you and just how much you belong on Cravenwood Block."

Something warmed inside my heart, I couldn't help it. I liked the sound of that. "Not gonna lie, that doesn't sound half bad."

———

GROCERIES WITH OLLIE turned out to be a comedic exercise in patience.

He was like a kid in a candy store one moment, and comparing prices by unit the next. He threw items into his cart with no rhyme or reason, but then he'd whip out coupons and search for exactly the right item in order to save a dollar.

"Are you seriously buying Raisin Bran?" Ollie asked me, wrinkling his nose as he perused my cart.

"I like it."

"And oatmeal? I've never had good oatmeal. It's always lumpy and tastes like paste." He made a gagging noise.

"I make good oatmeal."

"Is the bran cereal to keep the pooper healthy?" Ollie spoke easily as if he hadn't just mentioned my bowel habits in the middle of a small locally-owned grocery store.

Pinching the bridge of my nose, I chose to ignore the question.

"I get it. I take fiber supplements. I like the kind you mix with water best. In an apartment full of eight men—at least six of whom are gay or bi—we should probably buy stock in fiber supplements. Or at least shop in bulk for a good discount." Ollie pushed his cart as he spoke. "I'm not one hundred percent sure on top or bottom preference for everyone else—heck, maybe some are more sides than top or bottom, I really don't know—but I figure six out of eight being gay means at least a few are intent on keeping their guts cleaned out to make bedroom activities easily enjoyable. Ya know?"

"I don't often find myself thinking about the bowel health or bedroom activities of others," I mumbled.

"Really? I think about that shit a lot—haha, that pun wasn't intended, but it worked perfectly. I crack myself up most the time." He gestured toward a display and only at that moment did I realize we were in the sexual health section of the store. "I'd pass on the toys—better selection and quality at this online store I know. But condoms? Lube? I hear you've got a new roommate who is totally down with being professional by day and getting sexy at night."

"I'm not having sex with you, Oliver."

He pouted his lips. "That's a shame. But I notice you chose to say *I'm not having sex with you* rather than *I don't want to have sex with you* and that's a distinct difference in wording I'm definitely on board with."

"Either way," I said, "it ends in us not having sex."

"But saying you're not going to do something is easier

to deal with than hearing you don't *want* to do something." Ollie shrugged, a mischievous smile making his eyes sparkle. "I like knowing it's probably just some misplaced sense of professional duty or thinking you're too old for me or something. When I first realized you were my boss, I was devastated thinking nothing could happen between us—and also worried I was getting fired for offering to suck you off, thanks for being cool about that by the way. Now I realize, work can be work and home life can be home life. What we get up to at home is no one's business, right?"

"We're not getting up to anything, Oliver."

"But we *could*. I think there's a spark between us. I won't push the issue—"

I snorted. "This is you not pushing the issue?"

Ollie grinned. "Something like that. Anyway, I won't push it. I'm usually more like a dog with a bone, but I'm willing to let this play out naturally. I like you. I think you like me—if you'd let yourself just admit it. I think we could be really good together. I'd consider myself vers, with slightly more preference for bottoming." His cheeks flushed and his mouth moved as if he wanted to say more, but he just cleared his throat while grabbing lube and condoms.

Why was the universe out to get me? Why would it place me in a situation like this with a man like Ollie if not for the chance to destroy me?

The words and images he'd planted in my head were going to be the death of me. Not because I couldn't handle that kid in bed—I had every confidence we'd be perfectly compatible—but because I basically had to ignore his come-ons and the desperate urge to pull him close, shut him up, and show him just how good we could be.

But it was the right thing to do.

I was his boss.

Sure, we knew each other before I was his boss, so I wasn't technically taking advantage of my position, but still.

He was too young for me. In the grand scheme of things, I wasn't planning to settle down with him, so age wasn't a huge factor, even though it still confused me how I was even attracted to him when I'd always dated older-than-me men.

And honestly, getting involved with a roommate when I had no plans on being around for long seemed dicey at best. Devastating at worst.

Not like I was worried about my heart.

I'd never truly been in love and didn't expect it to happen now.

Randal and I were...well, I'd cared for him and thought we could have a pretty nice life together, but it was more playing at being the happy couple. Mostly for show. We got along fine. The sex was great. We looked good together.

But I hadn't handed him my heart—and that was a good thing since he turned out to be an asshole.

If I hadn't lost my heart to a long-term relationship, I seriously didn't think I'd have any heart issues with Ollie.

Maybe we could just play around for a year and then go our separate ways.

No.

I needed to stop that shit.

There were too many cons weighing against very few pros—the pros only being Ollie was adorably cute and fuckable, easy to talk to, and entertaining. Other than that, any involvement with him was a bad, bad idea.

I had to keep telling myself that.

———

WE FELL into an easy routine at the apartment and the education center over the next several weeks.

The seven men I lived with were great. It wasn't like I'd gotten to be close friends with any of them—schedules seldom ever matched and everyone had their own shit to do—but I knew I liked them better than almost any other people I'd ever known in my whole life.

Eight people living together could have easily been a tension-filled disaster, but we made it work. I think the combination of different ages, different schedules, new and established relationships, and the fact we weren't together twenty-four-seven helped.

And we also were respectful, responsible people.

The education center was truly great.

Maybe I didn't plan to stay on forever, but several weeks in had me believing a year would be simple.

It was very different from my past careers, but in a good way.

I had a lot of fun watching the children learning from amazing teachers, and the best part was we didn't have to answer to state or federal mandates since we were privately funded.

And I loved we didn't cater only to affluent families. Any kid who wanted to take classes at Cravenwood Education Center was able to thanks to sliding payments and scholarships.

Yes, we had a large number of very wealthy families who didn't even bat an eye at paying full-price for the additional education their children could receive from us —in fact, I'd caught on pretty quickly a lot of the families expected a high tuition as it made them feel it was the best *and* gave them something to brag about to their friends.

Each and every child who came to us deserved the best instruction we could give, but the children who were there because they wanted to be and not just because their parents wanted to pay for one more activity for them to be in were the ones I enjoyed watching the most.

Despite the fact I'd decided to dig into the center's past financial records—which was going to take some time —I still found time each day to greet parents and students as they came to morning and afternoon classes.

I made sure to be a visible presence in the hallways and classrooms—knowing from experience visibility from those in charge always made things feel more cohesive and run more efficiently.

My favorite time of day was when I could catch Ollie with students. Guitar in hand or seated at a keyboard, he was completely in his element when teaching children to appreciate music. Nothing was ever boring with Ollie—he somehow made music history and theory come to life, had kids understanding the importance of music in their lives within moments of their first class, and easily helped students to cope and reach for calm through rhythm, melody, lyrics, and movement.

Within the first month or so of being there, I realized my stress, apathy, exhaustion, and headaches of the past were no longer plaguing me as much.

Maybe it was the center.

Maybe it was my new living situation.

Maybe it was Ollie.

Probably a combination of all three.

But it was good and I was grateful.

Ollie turned out to be a lot different than my first impression of him.

He'd come across crass and over-the-top and somewhat annoying in his overexuberance, but he had a softer side as well.

He was dedicated to his job.

He was a loyal friend.

He was funny, caring, and easy to be around.

He was genuine—but not.

Genuine in that he really did love his job and his friends.

But he was covering up hurt, hiding pain from his past.

I wasn't sure *how* I knew—maybe years of working with teens and young adults—but I knew within the month of knowing him the jokes, the laughs, the inappropriate comments were a mask.

Sure, he really was funny and it was easy to laugh with him.

Yes, he had a right to say what he wanted.

And I did believe him when he indicated—almost too often—all the things he wanted to do with me in bed.

But there was a reason he did those things in the first place.

I wanted to pry and figure out the reason—ridiculously enough, I'd found myself attached to the man in ways I'd never expected or desired, and my head and heart weren't listening to my protests—but I also didn't want to know what had hurt him in the past.

My suspicions were confirmed on a Wednesday morning while several of us hurried around getting ready for work.

"Anyone want to do noodles with us tonight?" Leighton asked. "Jett has a late appointment and I'm covering a closing shift, but we can eat before that."

Julian and Shaw agreed to dinner.

Lucas and Dean were still asleep, but they likely had shifts that would take them away from noodles with the roomies.

"Sorry, can't. Gotta get my head examined," Ollie said with a wink.

I frowned, not wanting to put him on the spot right then and there.

As we headed down the stairs and out the door to the education center, I cleared my throat. "You have a doctor appointment? Headaches or something?"

Ollie chuckled. "Interesting and nosy question coming from someone who sneaks off every Wednesday evening and Sunday afternoon to an unknown location, comes back smelling of perfume—which is *not* a flattering scent, by the way—and expects none of us to wonder." He waved off my attempt at a protest. "I have a therapy appointment. My mom was pretty lackluster—and that's putting it politely—and my childhood messed me up. Things got better when I moved in with Julian and our dad, but therapy helps me work through some things."

"Gotcha. Sorry for prying." I felt like an ass.

Unlocking the door at the center, I flipped on the entryway lights.

"This is where you could divulge your own little secret," Ollie said.

He was right. Tit for tat and all of that.

I wasn't embarrassed of my Wednesday and Sunday trips. They were probably the best part of my week and I was grateful my new location allowed me twice a week now instead of just once.

But those were mine.

And I was greedy.

I didn't want to share.

I didn't want the good—no, the *best*—of my past to belong to anyone but me.

Maybe that was selfish, but I just wasn't ready.

So, like a child with a new toy, I shook my head. "Just things I have to do and those are the days I do them."

Ollie eyed me suspiciously. "Mmhm. This is me totally *not* believing you. You're a sneaky sneaker who sneaks and your lying skills are terrible." He pursed his lips. "I'll figure you out," he warned with a smile and a wag of his finger.

SEVEN

Ollie
___

BASH and I had been colleagues and roommates for about six weeks and I had the blue balls to prove it.

Okay, not really. I maybe wasn't getting off with Bash or anyone else, but I definitely wasn't abstaining from orgasms. Fingers, toys, and lube were my friends, despite how badly I wanted an actual dick inside me—an actual dick belonging to my boss if I was being specific.

Bash was...ugh, I wasn't even sure how to describe him.

He was professional and efficient at work, but still friendly and personable. The staff, students, and parents were in awe of him and had immediately joined Team Bash along with me—although, I was pretty sure I was the only one wanting to do dirty things with him.

At home, he was respectful and responsible. The eight of us all got along really well and I'd started thinking of us all as friends more than just roommates.

He pitched in and helped as if it was the most natural thing in the world.

He hung out, chatted and laughed, and pretty much seemed to enjoy himself.

Bash and I talked a lot. Like, *a lot*, but it was almost always pretty superficial. I mean, I knew he liked whiskey sours and bourbon—both of which I thought were gross and he laughed when he said my palate just wasn't as distinguished as his. He knew I was a huge fan of chocolate milk and he'd even throw a couple bottles in his cart for me when he went shopping.

Which, come on, *sigh* and heart eyes.

Bash seemed to like pretty much any food put in front of him, so we had that in common. He listened to a lot of different music from what I could tell, read a wide variety of books—maybe only slightly preferring mysteries—and enjoyed action dramas and a comedy here and there if he watched television.

He didn't seem to have anything but professional clothes—but he somehow distinguished between some of them as more casual than others. He laughed at my threadbare t-shirt I still held onto from my high school days and just shook his head with a soft smile when he saw my ripped jeans.

Like I said, most everything was fairly superficial.

We'd only gotten a bit past the surface-level stuff in the time we'd known each other.

He'd already told me about Randal cheating on him and a few other things he'd mentioned from time to time made me think he was more pissed than hurt—maybe like he missed the idea of having a long-term relationship more than he actually missed Randal.

I knew a bit about Caleb the college guy who made

false allegations. And after knowing Bash for like five minutes, I knew without a shadow of a doubt Caleb was a manipulative douche and I hoped I never ran into him because I'd for sure be giving him a piece of my mind. Not that I wasn't happy to have Bash around—and that really only happened because of Randal and Caleb—but lying about someone and costing them their job was a really shitty move.

So, I knew a few things about Bash, but I knew nothing about his childhood or his mysterious Wednesday and Sunday trips. On one hand, maybe those things weren't really my business. But on the other hand, I was desperate to know him, to know anything about him, to build on the connection I swore was between us.

I knew I wasn't imagining the way he looked at me—Leighton confirmed it, and even my brother couldn't deny Bash often looked at me like he wanted to devour me.

When I'd first seen him in the diner, I thought of him as nothing more than just a challenge, a fun time.

When I'd offered him the room, I'd thought maybe things could be a bit more.

When I'd realized he was my boss, I'd truly thought maybe things would crash and burn. Then I'd let myself hope we could keep work and personal lives separate.

After working with Bash, living with him, and getting to know him—albeit less than I wanted to—I'd come to realize I liked him more than just as a challenge or casual dating.

It was driving me insane that Bash was able to so easily keep me at arm's length.

He was doing to me what I'd always done to others and I didn't love it.

Being in a situation where I wanted something more than just quick and easy fun was new to me—thanks to dear ol' Mom for teaching me how to flit from guy to guy, never opening myself to love because I didn't believe I was worthy.

The feelings I had for Bash were new to me.

And Bash didn't seem at all inclined to get involved.

I think the most aggravating thing was knowing he was attracted to me, but he wasn't willing to give in to the attraction because I was young, we worked together, and he wasn't going to be around long.

Blah.

Blah.

Blah.

If only I could have talked him into the friends-with-benefits situation Leighton and Jett had going on.

Instead, I was stuck getting myself off in the shower and fucking myself with my fingers and toys while I lay in bed imagining Bash on the other side of the thin wall.

If I'd thought the attraction was unrequited, I would have thrown in the towel and moved on.

But my gut told me Bash liked me.

I just wasn't sure how to get him to give in to it.

One Sunday afternoon, Bash popped his head into my room. "I'm heading out. See you in the morning if you're in bed by the time I get home." The eight of us had taken to making sure at least one person knew where we were going to be if we weren't working or at home.

I narrowed my eyes at him, dying to know where his

Wednesday and Sunday trips took him, but just nodded. "Yeah, see ya. Have fun…doing whatever or whoever it is you sneak off to do."

Bash rolled his eyes. "Enjoy your afternoon, Oliver."

I grunted.

Five minutes later, because I hadn't yet heard the door close *and* because I'd decided to go visit my father, I pulled on a pair of shoes and left my room.

Bash was just pocketing his phone and keys as he grabbed a bottle of water from the fridge.

Pushing up beside him, purposely getting in his space because I was feeling feisty and bratty, I reached around to get a bottle of chocolate milk. Bash tensed and I smiled, sneaking a soft breath of him—something that reminded me of lemon, sage, and leather—as I whispered at his ear, "Thought you were leaving."

Bash took a deep breath, schooling himself before answering, "I am. Just needed to check some email and grab a water."

"Better get going then," I murmured, still pressed against him, the fridge standing open, knowing I was pushing my luck.

"I'm going."

"Feel free to wake me up when you get home," I suggested, fighting the urge to drop my mouth to his neck to nibble and suck. "But not if you're coming home from being with someone else. I've not been in any long-term or serious relationships…" *Or any relationships at all* I thought to myself, "…but I've recently realized I don't think I'm the type who can share a man with someone else."

Bash's hand brushed against mine and for a brief moment I thought he was maybe going to take my hand in his. "I'm not meeting up with another man, and I doubt I'll wake you up when I get home. We've got work early tomorrow."

"Is it a woman? You switching teams?" I frowned, stepping away from him and letting the fridge door close. "Huh, I guess I'd just assumed you're gay, my bad. Are you bi? Pan?"

Bash huffed. "I'm gay. I'm not hooking up with anyone. I gotta go."

"Why can't you just tell me where you go? You're mean and you get way too much enjoyment out of driving me insane." I took a long swig of chocolate milk, not missing the way Bash's eyes caught on my throat with each swallow.

He chuckled. "I don't do it on purpose, you just make it too easy." Cocking his head to the side, he continued, "It wasn't meant to be a big secret, and it's not anything earth shattering, I'm just not sure I'm ready to share."

"Are you like a super hero? Fighting Cravenwood crime…" I wrinkled my nose, "…only on Wednesdays and Sundays? Okay, that's stupid. Do you go watch movies by yourself? That's kinda cool—but makes me jealous because I'd like to get cozy at a Sunday matinee with you." My brain struggled trying to come up with anything he might be doing on his secret trips. "Do you do nude modeling for an art school? Work at a soup kitchen? Take Pilates classes? Learn how to crochet?"

"You have a very active imagination. As fun as it would

be to hear you continue your wild guesses, I need to go. See you tomorrow."

"Well, have fun," I said, doing my best not to pout.

Bash made his way out the door and I went to let Leighton know I was leaving. The noises coming from his room indicated he was highly preoccupied, so I opted to text him to let him know I was going to visit my dad.

Julian and I saw Dad quite often since he lived and worked nearby.

Roger Johnson had gotten mixed up with my mother several years after Julian's mother had passed away from a heart condition. Tonya Barrows, my brother's mom, had never married Roger, but they'd had several good years together before she'd died when Julian was about eight-years-old.

My understanding from the bit Dad had shared was he and my mom got tangled up when he ran into her begging for drug money at a gas station. He tried to help her—gave her a place to stay for a while.

Mom wasn't a *bad* person, just made a lot of bad choices and never could escape her demons. I vividly recall her talking about how Roger Johnson was the best thing that ever happened to her and could have been the love of her life if she hadn't fucked it up.

They started an intimate relationship, Mom got pregnant with me, but she bailed before I was born. Roger had Julian to look after and he lost track of her, mainly because she didn't want him knowing where she was—she took off and shacked up with men who didn't care if she was doing drugs or taking care of herself and her son.

When I was eight, she dropped me off at Roger's place.

Nineteen-year-old Julian had answered the door and seen me standing there—dirty, exhausted, and unsure. Roger had come to the door, taken one look at me, glanced over my shoulder to give Mom a quick, hard nod, and ushered me inside.

My life had changed that day.

I'd lost a mother—but had I ever really had her?

She'd left me with years of trauma to unpack and work through, but she'd given me to Dad and Julian and that had been the best thing ever.

For the first time in my life, I wasn't hungry or dirty or scared.

Julian had taken me under his wing immediately.

Dad had promised I'd never again wonder where I was sleeping or getting food.

I was safe.

When I finally got up the nerve to tell Julian I was gay —he'd recently come out himself in his late twenties—I knew my dad and brother loved me, but I was still terrified Roger wouldn't want me around. I was nearing eighteen and I told myself I'd be fine on my own.

But Dad turned out to be the most over-the-top, supportive parent ever. Roger Johnson was a giant of a man—neither Julian or I looked very much like him, both of us taking more after our mothers—but he was a soft teddy bear. He immediately joined PFLAG, read everything he could get his hands on regarding how to be a parent to queer youth, educated himself on gay sex, and marched in any and every Pride parade and function he could find.

Just like the day he'd taken me in without question,

Dad had accepted me for who I was without even batting an eye. He'd saved me in more ways than one and I loved him dearly for it, even when he was somewhat embarrassing in my teen years. He loved nothing more than pointing out guys I might think were hot, but he also felt the need to give detailed demonstrations of how to use a dental dam, how to put on a condom, which lube was best, and the safest way to prepare for anal sex.

He'd taken me to my first clinic appointment when I told him I'd been giving blow jobs. He bought me condoms and lube, recommended a helpful video for anal sex preparation, insisted I get on PrEP, and hung a rainbow flag on the porch. I drew the line when he wanted to buy me a butt plug and dildo, but I couldn't talk him out of at least going to the sex shop with me to browse the aisles.

Yeah, Dad was over-the-top supportive, but I knew Julian and I were beyond lucky to have him. From what he'd said, Tonya would have supported Julian no matter what. I wasn't sure about my own mother, and honestly, I was glad I never had to find out.

There was a void in my life where my mother had once been, but having Dad and Julian had helped fill it—I honestly believed I was better off without her, even if it meant sometimes longing for a mother-son relationship I never had.

As I stepped onto the sidewalk to head toward the Midtown Retirement Community where Dad worked as the head physical therapist, I glanced down the block and realized I wasn't far behind Bash.

Shit.

The urge to follow him and see just where he went on his twice-a-week excursions was strong.

But that felt wrong.

No, I'd just keep on my normal path to see my Dad before his shift ended for the day. If Bash was going the same way, I couldn't help that. If he took a different way, I wouldn't follow him.

As I walked, I wondered about Bash. He seemed pretty upfront about most everything, I figured he'd tell me if he had a lover—even if just to get me to back off. But what else would he keep secret?

My interest was beyond piqued when Bash continued on in the exact same direction as me turn after turn. The only other thing besides the retirement community in that direction was big box warehouse. Did he work there? He didn't appear to need extra money—I'd gotten hints maybe Caleb's false allegations provided him with some extra financial padding—and Bash most definitely wasn't dressed for work in warehouse, although his ass looked *fine* in his designer jeans. I couldn't help but laugh at the difference between Bash's take on *casual* versus mine—I was sporting black joggers and a hoodie.

I sped up, wanting to make sure I saw where he turned. Maybe there was more in this direction than I realized.

When he walked into the retirement home, I couldn't help muttering, "What the hell?" and running to follow him inside.

What happened next was like a slow-motion scene from a movie.

Right in the middle of the foyer, Sebastian Evans was shaking my dad's hand.

What? They knew each other?

Did Bash know someone at the home?

Dad caught sight of me and beamed, waving enthusiastically as was his nature.

Bash caught sight of me and frowned, anger blazing over his face as I made my way toward them.

"Ollie!" Dad called out, still smiling.

"Oliver," Bash grumbled.

"Didn't know you were coming," Dad said, pulling me into a hug.

"Did you follow me?" Bash hissed.

The three of us stood in a small circle, tension and confusion thick between Bash and me, oblivious happiness on my dad's part.

"Oh, do you two know each other?" Dad asked, glancing between Bash and me. "Not that I'm still under the impression every gay man knows each other," he said quietly to just me as if Bash wasn't standing right there.

I pinched the bridge of my nose, somewhat understanding why Bash and Julian did the same *often* around me and my lack of filter.

"Why are you here?" Bash demanded.

"Why are *you* here?" I asked right back.

Dad eyed the two of us with amused curiosity. "Bash," he started, "this is my son."

Bash's eyes grew wide, but he covered his surprise quickly. "You're Oliver's father? And Julian's?" When Dad nodded proudly, Bash smiled sheepishly. "Small world, huh?" He glanced my way. "Sorry, that was rude and presumptuous to accuse you of following me."

"Apology accepted. Not that it didn't cross my mind for a moment when I first realized I was behind you." I turned to Dad. "Bash is my new boss and roommate."

Dad rubbed his hands together chuckling. "Well, if that doesn't sound like the beginning of a tale that's yet to be completely penned."

Bash's cheeks actually pinked. "Nothing like that, I assure you."

Dad winked. "Mmhm." He waved a hand toward a hallway of apartments. "She had a really good session today and she's excited to see you as always."

I glanced between Dad and Bash, dying to ask just who they were talking about. I knew Dad couldn't discuss patients and Bash hadn't seemed to want me to know anything about this person before.

He must have seen something on my face because Bash sighed. "Fine. She'll want to meet you since you're Roger's son, and we both know you'll hound me at home until I finally break." He rolled his eyes, but the little smirk told me he wasn't actually mad. Something weird fluttered in my stomach when Bash referred to our place as *home*. "My aunt LuLu lives here. Let me prepare her, she'll be in a tizz over having an extra guest. I'll text you the apartment number here in a bit. Visit with your dad."

My heart flip-flopped.

No.

There was no reason to be giddy about meeting Bash's aunt.

It likely would have never happened if we hadn't ended up at the same place at the same time.

He wasn't introducing me because he *wanted* to, it was just a logical step because of them both knowing my dad.

I mean, Bash could have disappeared down the hall to visit LuLu and never told me a single bit of information. So, it was nice he was letting me in on his secret person.

But it definitely wasn't like he was introducing me because there was anything between us.

Right?

"Can't say he's ever introduced anyone to LuLu," Dad murmured beside me, tearing me from my thoughts but most definitely not helping. "She's been here five years. He never brought anyone to meet her—not even that lowlife cheating man he used to be with."

"We're friends and I happened upon his secret, that's all," I muttered.

Dad eyed me, lips pursed. "Yeah, okay. Secret may not be accurate. He's very protective, but I don't know that LuLu is *secret*, maybe just he doesn't like to share his time with her. They're close." He made a show of locking his lips and tossing the key. "And that's all I can say about that."

I chuckled, nervous about meeting Bash's aunt.

"How long have you been pining over this guy?" Dad asked. "And don't think I don't realize he's several years older than you...if I didn't already know the type of person he is, I'd be concerned. But Bash is a good guy."

"I'm not pining," I protested.

"Yeah, okay," Dad repeated with a smile and an eye roll. "I've seen you with your flavors of the week—

sometimes of the *day*—and I've heard you talk about guys you've been chasing. Never once in all the years since you came out to me and I became a ferocious, rainbow flying Papa Bear—"

"Dear god, don't ever call yourself Papa Bear in my presence ever again," I interrupted.

Dad laughed. "My point being, you've never had this glow, this energy," he waved his hand toward me, "with other guys. Bash has you all heart-eyes and fluttery, looking at him like you want him to eat you alive and start in on building a white picket fence."

I shook my head. "He's different. But it doesn't matter, he's not around for long. Plus, he's *all* sorts of caught up on the fact I'm younger, he's my boss, and we're roommates. I'm all for it, but I don't think he's going to let it happen."

Dad laughed again. "We'll see. Sometimes our best intentions don't go as planned. Just like I've never seen *you* all aflutter like this, I've never seen Bash so...I can't exactly put my finger on it, but he's definitely different. He looks at you like I've never seen—"

When I started to protest, Dad just raised a hand.

"I'm just saying, don't give up if you think it could be something good." Dad put an arm around me. "You deserve the best and I trust Bash."

"He's leaving," I said.

"So he says. I also thought I was going to move on to bigger and better when I started here so many years ago." He jostled me against his side. "And look at me now. Your brother thought managing the apartments would be a stepping stone, but now I don't think we could pay him enough to leave."

"You really see something between us?" I asked.

"I do," Dad said with a nod. "You're both different around each other—I noticed it the moment I saw you together—but also, your personalities seem to just mesh. Kinda like you balance each other out. The real test will be to see what LuLu thinks."

My eyes darted to Dad's face. "What? Why? Oh god, is she terrifying? You think she won't like me? Old people usually like me—I think. I mean, Bash didn't exactly like me in the beginning, but that was because I offered to—"

Dad's raised eyebrow made my words come to a screeching halt.

Chuckling, I waved it away. "Never mind, and he's not even old. Point is, I won him over with my charming personality. Is LuLu going to be more of a challenge?"

Dad laughed. "LuLu is a hoot. She's the reason Bash is who he is. That's their story to tell, but I think you'll like her. If she sees the same thing between the two of you I do, she'll be on your side in a heartbeat." He slapped my back. "Now, I'm heading out for cards and beer with my buddies. You and Julian need to come over soon, we'll grill out."

"That sounds good," I said. "Or you could come to our place. We're making plans for parties on the roof."

"Fun times. I'll be there."

I hugged my dad goodbye just as my phone buzzed.

Bash: *Apartment 5B*

. . .

WITH A BALL of unexpected nerves bouncing in my belly, I headed toward Bash and his aunt. My head was full of uncertainty which was slightly unusual for me in most situations. It was the unknown—and the fact I wanted to make a good impression. Despite Bash being so adamant nothing could happen between us, I felt something there and I swore it wasn't one-sided.

If I got LuLu on my side, maybe Bash would see he could give us a chance. Even if just a date. Or just sex. True, I selfishly wanted more—and that was such a trip to wrap my head around—but I wasn't against starting small.

Goal one—get LuLu on my side.

Goal two—keep at it and wear Bash down until he finally took me out or at least took me to bed.

I winced. Okay, there were some obstacles I'd need to bring to light in the bedroom situation, but we had to get to that point first. If I brought it up too soon, Bash would likely run far, far away.

Goal three—keep reminding myself Bash had no plans to stick around. I needed to protect my heart. I'd never once allowed myself to get close enough or enamored enough to have to worry about my heart.

But Bash was different.

Wiping my sweaty hands on my pants, I knocked at 5B.

The door opened and Bash stood on the other side, his face wary, eyes drilling into mine. We stared at each other for a ridiculously long time and I got the distinct feeling Bash was both nervous and excited.

Something about the moment told me it was a pivotal point.

"Hey," Bash finally said, stepping aside to let me in.

"Is that him? The boy who has my nephew all discombobulated?" LuLu called from somewhere in the apartment.

Bash pinched the bridge of his nose. Huh, I guess that wasn't a gesture reserved *only* for dealing with me.

"Well, bring him in here," LuLu said again. "It's about time I meet the man who can get you all twisted up."

Bash gestured through a tiny kitchen, ushering me toward the living room, his hand on the small of my back making my insides warm.

An older woman, possibly around seventy, beamed at me from...uhhhh, a tiny trampoline? What the hell?

Dressed in a black and pink windbreaker type jogging suit, LuLu bounced on a small circular trampoline in the corner of her living room, a sweatband around her head to hold short, spiky gray hair from her forehead. In her hands she held small dumbbells which couldn't have weighed more than two pounds each, but at her age, maybe that was enough.

I hadn't had much time to form of picture of LuLu in my head, but *this* wasn't what I'd been expecting. Shawls, knitting, daytime soaps, crossword puzzles, and prune juice danced through my head as I tried to reconcile the image in front of me. Yeah, I'd been prepared for dentures in a cup, maybe a walker, and a stuffy, hot apartment that smelled like mothballs.

I was confident in myself to admit when I'd fallen victim to stereotyping and I'd been wrong.

So very wrong.

"LuLu, this is my roommate, Oliver Mayer," Bash said,

a hint of mischief in his smile. "Oliver, this is my aunt LuLu." He glanced back and forth between us as if just realizing something then he groaned. "You're both absolute menaces, so you should get along just fine," he said with a huff.

"It's Ollie," I said, shooting daggers at Bash. "It's nice to meet you. I'd like to say I've heard so much about you, but until about twenty minutes ago, I didn't know you existed."

LuLu stopped bouncing and stepped off the trampoline to make her way toward me. "Girl, same," she said with a grin. "Oh, I like this one." She patted my face and nodded, throwing a wink Bash's way. "Ollie, come sit. Tell me about yourself."

We made a bit of small-talk about jobs and hobbies. I learned LuLu used to be a dietician, but she also smoked a lot of pot, did Jazzercise, played the guitar, and painted abstract art.

She was possibly the coolest old person I'd ever met.

Maybe the coolest person I'd ever met, period.

No wonder Bash wanted to keep her to himself.

"I like to stay fit and active," she said, motioning toward the trampoline. "That father of yours keeps me in tip-top shape with his exercises. Good man that Roger." She waggled a finger at Bash. "While *this* one has kept pretty quiet about his gorgeous new love interest—"

Bash nearly choked on his water. "No. Just no."

LuLu ignored him. "While Bash hasn't said much, I've heard all about you and your brother from your father for years."

I beamed. I knew my father loved my brother and me, but hearing he talked so highly of us when we weren't around always made my insides swirly and warm.

"So, let me tell you a bit about this one," LuLu said, gesturing toward Bash.

"Can we not? Please?" Bash asked on a groan. It was fascinating to me how he'd gone from this sophisticated, closed-off, serious man to basically a whining, petulant teen in the presence of his aunt—I loved seeing a different side to him and I pretty much already loved the woman who had brought him down to that level.

"Hush." LuLu gave him a wink. "Bash is my sister's son. My sister and I were as different as night and day. Sadly, she died, but not until after raising this one to age ten and giving him enough baggage to last a life time. His father was no better. When my sister died, Bash's dad basically forgot he had a son. I swooped in and took Bash to live with me." She leaned in and pretended to whisper, "He's always taken a while to loosen up. He comes across as a stick-in-the-mud fuddy-duddy at times, but he's got a heart of gold and he's a *good* person. Terrible taste in men up until now, but maybe his luck is changing."

"Dear lord, this is my worst nightmare," Bash grumbled. "Why are you like this?"

"I'm a combo of loving, caring, supportive mother and wild, crazy, beat-of-her-own-drum aunt. I'm not getting any younger. One day, I'll pass on," LuLu gestured absently with a hand, "and I want to know you're loved and cared for when I'm gone."

"I'm not a damn dog needing a place to live when you're dead—not that I think you're going anywhere anytime soon, you'll outlive us all on a cocktail of pot and sparkling spring water."

LuLu cackled. "I've moved on to butterfly pea flower tea and kombucha, but you're probably right."

"Oh my god," I piped up. "You like butterfly pea flower tea? It's my favorite."

LuLu clapped her hands together and smiled broadly. "I *knew* I liked you. Let's have some tea while we talk."

Bash sank back into his seat on the couch as if resigned for this visit to be long and miserable.

Fifteen minutes later, LuLu and I had our tea and were discussing the best brands and places to buy it.

"You *must* come to dinner on Wednesday. Bash and I have been having Sunday and Wednesday dinners ever since he came to live with me. He was a timid kid, always tucking away his emotions and fighting against the fear of people not wanting him around." LuLu patted Bash's knee. "I think that's why he settled for that dreadful Randal—the relationship provided a sense of stability, but he never really had to get emotionally involved." She turned to me. "What about you, Ollie? What kind of emotional trauma do you bring to the table?"

I snorted. "Let's just say I'd definitely need a bell boy if I wanted to carry it all."

"I've gotten that impression from your dad," LuLu said. "But I've also been told you're successful and about as well-balanced as one can expect to be when a mother abandoned them."

My eyes shot to Bash, both of us seeming to realize at the same moment we had a lot more in common than sharing an apartment and working together.

"I lucked out being sent to live with Dad and Julian, that's for sure. I have a great job—pretty kick-ass new boss—" I winked at Bash. "—and a great group of friends. Having a deadbeat mom and moving from one couch to another each month as she flitted through her hookups and drug money wasn't the best foundation, but Dad is amazing and he helped a lot. Once I got that stability, things got a lot better." Taking the opportunity to let Bash in on a few things, I continued, "Sure, I still have Mom's habit of flitting and never getting too involved, but I think the right person will come along and change that at some point."

LuLu held fingers to her lips. "Sebastian Thomas, if you don't take this boy home and proclaim your undying love for him—preferably in your bed—I'm going to wonder if I failed in my attempts to raise you." She shook her head, ignoring Bash's strangled protests. "I'd always hoped the day would finally come where my nephew met his match. And here you are." She reached out and took my hand. "You boys can't tell me this isn't the perfect example of fate intervening to bring two people together. Working together, living together—"

"Those are just circumstances," Bash interrupted. "In fact, they're things that could potentially derail a relationship—not that there *is* a relationship…"

"You're right. Those two things in and of themselves aren't enough. But there's more to it." LuLu nodded. "You two might not see it—one of you might try to put on blinders—but there's a reason the two of you met." She clapped her hands in front of her chest. "And I'm pleased as punch to be here to watch it unfold. When's the next time you're going out? Maybe I could tag along."

Bash made a noise like someone had spooned out his liver. "No. You're not going anywhere with us."

Biting my lip, I tried to hide a smile when Bash realized what he'd said and held his face in his hands. "Bash hasn't taken me out yet," I said with a pout. "Remember?" I stage-whispered. "He thinks it's a bad idea for us to get involved. Age, being my boss, he's not sticking around, blah, blah, blah."

LuLu nodded sagely. "Ohhhh, right," she whispered back, playing along. Truly, this was the most fun I'd had in a long time. "Well, we'll just have to let him think he's got it all under control. Age is just a number. You knew each other *before* he became your boss. As for the sticking around part, we'll just see about that. Maybe if he has his poor aging aunt *and* his love interest in Cravenwood, he'll be more tempted. Plus, even when he wasn't living and working on Cravenwood Block, he's lived in or around Midtown his whole life. I don't see him going far."

Bash scowled, looking as if he wanted to strangle LuLu.

I smiled, a surge of hope filling my chest when I realized, even if Bash moved out and left the education center, he likely wasn't moving across the country. His *I'm leaving* excuse had just been shot full of holes.

LuLu took both our hands. "Our minds and emotions are such interesting things. You both have such similar pasts and you deal with things in similar ways. If I were a fortune teller, I'd be rubbing all over my pretty glass ball and saying things like, 'I see a stable, loving relationship in your future,' and 'You're on your way to finding your forever, you just have to open your mind. And your heart.'" LuLu chuckled at Bash's eye roll. "Now, let's make sure we're on the same page. Bash is vers but often prefers to top. Ollie?"

I swallowed my tongue. "Um, what?"

"Jesus," Bash mumbled, a pathetic whine leaving him. "No."

"Are you vers? Bottom?" LuLu persisted.

Oh. My. God.

"Oh, um. Vers. Probably lean a bit more toward bottom?" I mean, I wasn't lying. I definitely enjoyed fingers and toys in my ass. Just because they'd always been put there by me didn't mean I probably wouldn't like it if someone—namely, Bash—put his dick in me.

Okay, time to stop that line of thinking.

Getting a boner in front of Bash and LuLu would be an over-the-top awkward ending to an already weirdly fascinating and amazing encounter.

"Perfect. Definitely compatible in bed." LuLu stood and took our tea cups to the kitchen. "Sex is usually the easy part—at least in my experience...I'll have to tell you about my sexual escapades sometime." She chuckled when Bash made a strangled noise and looked as if he wanted the ground to swallow him up. "It's the emotional attachment that's harder. But I see the spark between the two of you. Go out, spend time together, let things happen. You like each other, it's obvious. Shame my nephew needed his elderly aunt to intervene—and just think how long it would have taken if fate hadn't brought you both here today...this has been years and years in the making, I just know it. Don't worry about age." She directed her words to Bash. "Don't worry about being his boss. Don't worry about whether or not you want to stay at that job. Focus on the way he makes your heart flutter. The way you smile more when he's around. The fact you'd like to hold his hand and wrap him in a warm embrace. How good his ass looks in a pair of skin-tight jeans."

Bash choked on air.

I preened. "Why, thank you."

LuLu chuckled. "I've got a bunch of old biddies to beat at cards this evening, so I'm going to need to herd you on your way." She took my hand and pulled me from the couch. "I want to see more of you. I'll get your number from Bash so we can keep in touch." She leaned in close. "He's stubborn. Once he gets something in his head, it's hard to sway him. But when he finally lets go and allows himself to love, it's going to be spectacular. Don't stop fighting for his heart."

I swallowed a lump in my throat. What had started out as just a fun offer to suck off a hot older guy had turned into more than I'd ever thought possible. I wanted Bash in my life and I was willing to fight for him.

Yeah, that realization had my head reeling, and my heart protesting in hopes of not getting smashed to smithereens, but the exhilaration was like nothing I'd ever experienced.

"Bash, I wanted to talk to you for a second if you can wait just a bit. Tell Ollie you'll see him at home." LuLu gave me a final hug.

I gave Bash a tiny smile and wave and headed out the door.

"See you at home," Bash managed. "I need to start the paperwork for this one to be moved to solitary confinement. Or better yet, moved to the convalescent center." His words held no heat and I knew from his resigned smile and her mischievous smirk they teased each other often, and Bash felt no real anger with his aunt.

I made my way from LuLu's toward my place, my heart throbbing as I recalled Bash speaking of our *home*. Would LuLu's apparent approval of me be enough to sway Bash? I didn't know if I could imagine a time when he would just lay aside his reasons for keeping me at arm's length, but maybe LuLu had a lot more influence than I realized. He'd certainly been different around her—I liked to think the Bash I'd seen at LuLu's was the real man, and the one I'd been living and working with was hiding behind willfully erected barriers.

Don't get me wrong. I understood the barriers. People with a past like Bash and me often found ourselves putting up shields and walls to protect our hearts and minds from the painful pasts and any potential pain in the future.

Bash: I'm really sorry about that. I love her dearly, but she has no filter.

Me: No wonder we get along. No worries, she's great.

. . .

Bash: *She's something.*

Me: *It's so crazy to me that you and LuLu know my dad. He really likes her.*

Bash: *Your dad is great. I'd never put two and two together, but you and Julian are a lot like him.*

Me: *He is. We're lucky.*

BASH DIDN'T TEXT AGAIN.

I wondered if the fact he and LuLu knew my father was a pro or con toward Bash eventually admitting he felt something for me and allowing the spark to grow.

I got home and retreated to my room when I realized everyone was either out or holed-up in their own rooms as we all prepared for another work week.

Flopping down on my bed, I couldn't help the huge grin on my face.

Meeting LuLu had been amazing. She was like a mom, aunt, grandma, and bestie all rolled into one and I wanted to spend time with her and be her favorite. We'd have picnics where she sipped kombucha and I enjoyed my chocolate milk. She'd share her pot while we bonded over our adoration of Bash. She'd buy me a shirt that said *My*

LuLu Spoils Me and I'd totally wear it. The woman was outstanding and I wanted to bask in her presence.

I completely understood why Bash spent so much time with her and wanted to keep her to himself.

But the cat was out of the bag now and there was no stopping the Ollie and LuLu alliance. The fact she saw something between Bash and me warmed my heart and spurred me on in my continued attempt to wear the man down.

I'd seen the attraction, the longing on his face when we were together. I'd also seen the sheer stubbornness it took to keep from reaching out and hauling me close the way we both wanted, even if he refused to admit it.

Maybe with LuLu's welcomed interference—okay, welcomed at least on my part—Bash would finally let go of some of his stubbornness and let things happen between us. Truly, I wasn't asking for forever—I guess I was slowly coming around to the fact I didn't *hate* the idea of an actual future with Bash—but at least giving us a chance appealed. Greatly.

Closing my eyes, I pictured Bash. I adored so much about the man. His floppy hair and trimmed scruff, those dark eyes, his inability to wear anything that didn't look like he'd just walked out of GQ. He was intelligent, sophisticatedly funny, and caring. While he often came across as aloof, I'd realized quickly it just took him time to get comfortable and let people in. Bash maybe hadn't *meant* to, but he'd already shown me how much he cared for his students in the way he'd interacted with them just during the short amount of time he'd been at the center.

It was no wonder I'd found myself so infatuated. If the

initial physical attraction hadn't snared me, the resulting emotional attachment that came from living and working together would have done me in.

Of course, none of that would have happened if Bash had turned out to be a complete asshole. LuLu was right, Bash was good down to his core. The idea of being with him had my body on fire and expectation coursing through me.

Caressing my hand down my abs, I took my quickly thickening cock in my fist with a groan. I needed to get off and the images of Bash floating through my head were the perfect fodder.

Quickly stripping, I tossed my clothes on the floor and grabbed a used towel to spread on my bed. Yanking open my bedside table, I pulled out a dildo and bottle of lube, my dick twitching as a bead of precum escaped in anticipation.

With my imagination going buck wild, I suctioned the dildo to my headboard—it had taken plenty of practice to figure out just the right height, but I was now a pro—and pumped lube onto my fingers. Positioning myself in the center of the mattress, ass pointing toward the phallus stuck to the headboard, I straightened the towel before reaching between my legs and slicking my hole.

Knowing from experience just how much stretching I needed in order to take the silicone shaft with only the most enjoyable twinge of discomfort, I worked myself open. Imagining Bash's fingers in my ass, his hands all over me, his lips devouring me, I shivered and moaned.

Adding a bit more lube, I stroked the excess onto my dick before shifting back to line up the dildo with my ass.

I'd purposely gotten a realistically-sized toy for this particular position so I could take it without much trouble. Sure, there were times I wanted to gasp as I nearly split myself open, but this position wasn't one of those times.

With my knees spread open and my feet wedged in the space between the headboard and the bed, I rocked back, whimpering as I fucked myself onto the dildo, my body opening bit by bit as the toy sank into my ass.

I dropped to my elbows and arched my back, loving the slow, gentle slide of the silicone in and out of my tight muscle as I rocked on my knees. Reaching for my cock, I stroked myself while closing my eyes and picturing Bash behind me, thrusting his hips, fucking me open, hitting my prostate over and over again.

"Holy fuck," a strained voice whispered gruffly from the doorway.

My eyes flew open, head whipping to my very unlocked and open door.

Bash.

I froze, my ass begging for more and my cock throbbing in my hand.

"Don't stop," he choked out, cupping the bulge in the front of his pants.

As if I could.

With only the slightest falter in my movements, I resumed rocking on my knees, the slick glide of silicone in and out of my body making me quiver and moan, my eyes never leaving Bash.

Was this really happening? Or had I traveled too far into my imagination?

But our eyes met and held.

Fire crackling between us.

A war raged on Bash's face.

He wanted to leave.

Regretted being there in the first place.

But longing and desire gripped him. Attraction and want held him fast, refusing to let him walk away.

Every single emotion played out on his face.

And I could totally work with that.

Arching my back more, I shoved myself back on the dildo—sending up a silent prayer this was not the time when the fake phallus opted to unsuction itself from my headboard—moaning Bash's name.

I was a mostly-confident, successful adult, but girl, let me tell you something, I wasn't too proud to beg. If putting on an unrehearsed show—porning myself out to the best of my amateur ability—was what it took to *finally* get Bash to touch me, I was gonna porn myself like no one had ever porned before.

Yeah, yeah, I know. None of that really made sense, but let's not get distracted.

"Touch yourself," I said, eyeing his hand fighting not to stroke over his erection. "Take your dick out. Stroke yourself and imagine it's you in my ass."

As if in a trance, Bash unzipped his pants and shoved down his underwear. I nearly swallowed my tongue when his long, thick cock sprang out. Regret and desire swam over his face as he stroked himself.

Between the dildo in my ass brushing over my prostate when I got the angle just right and the sexiest hand job I'd ever witnessed in my life taking place right in front of me, I knew I wasn't going to last long.

I needed more.

Wanted to feel his touch.

Breathe him in.

Taste him.

"Come here," I demanded, never stopping the backward thrusts of my ass.

Bash's eyes closed, a pained expression filling his face as he fought to ignore my words.

"Bash, please. I'm dying over here. Come. Here," I rasped out, begging for what I knew we both wanted.

He pushed away from the doorframe—I had only a split-second to hope the outside door to our room was locked and no one came through the bathroom...oh well, if they did, they were going to get a show.

Bash made his way toward the bed, never taking his eyes off me, stroking his cock in slow, lazy passes as if trying to prolong the inevitable.

My mouth watered for a taste of him as I fucked myself while propped on bent elbows, my legs spread and hard cock begging for release. "Get on the bed," I ordered, wondering where the bossiness had come from when all I really wanted to do was roll over and give myself to Bash heart and soul.

Bash shook his head, his eyes saying he shouldn't, even as every movement screamed how badly he wanted to.

"Bash, please. Get on the bed. Give me this. Give *us* this," I rasped out.

Indecision and lust battled it out on Bash's face, and I saw the moment his desire won out.

His desire.

For me.

Holy shit, if that wasn't a heady feeling.

Bash shoved his pants and underwear to his ankles, stepping out of one leg, and climbed onto the mattress. With one hand still stroking his long, thick cock, Bash ran a hand through my hair, pressing against the back of my neck so I looked up at him as he brushed a thumb over my lips almost reverently.

As badly as I wanted him to get on my level and kiss me, the sight of his cock right in front of my face pushed me toward more pressing matters. "Give it to me," I demanded.

For a moment, I thought he was going to refuse.

Shake his head and get off the bed.

Tuck himself away and take a piece of me with him when he left.

Instead, Bash thumbed over his slit before smearing the head of his cock over my lips. The taste and scent were overwhelming and my senses short-circuited as I lapped at his leaking cock head, savoring the flavor, fighting between wanting to devour him and making it last.

Opening for him, spreading my lips wide to take him in, I groaned around his thick shaft as Bash slid to the back of my throat with a grunt.

The sensations of a toy up my ass, a cock teasing my gag reflex, and Bash's hand fisting in my hair was enough to send me into overload. I pressed my tongue to the underside of his cock, whimpering as he tightened his hold on my hair, and rocked harder and faster on the dildo.

We found the most perfect rhythm and I lost myself to the moment. When Bash's thrusting hips faltered and his grip on my hair had my eyes watering, I reached to fondle his balls. Finding them swollen and tight, knowing he was close, I took him deeper to the back of my throat and pressed a finger against his taint.

Bash tried to pull away with a strangled whisper that he was close, but I gripped his ass in one hand and forced him forward, taking every drop he gave me as his cock exploded in my mouth. With his load coating my tongue in hot spurts, my ass clenched around the silicone, I came hard and fast, making a mess of the towel but saving myself from a load of laundry.

I knew the moment Bash came back to earth because he made a pained noise and moved from the mattress, yanking his pants up, and eyeing me like a wary animal.

"I wanted that as much as you did, don't go getting weird," I warned him. "Let's talk."

Bash shook his head. "I'm sorry. That should have never happened. Fuck, Oliver, I'm so sorry."

And with that—no deep lingering kisses, no post-orgasmic smiles and tangle of limbs—Bash rushed from my room leaving me in a haze of confusion and worry tinged with hope.

———

I WOKE the next morning with a weird mishmash of awkwardness and elation zinging through me.

On one hand, everything that had taken place the night before had me ecstatic and hoping for the best. On the other hand, I couldn't imagine Bash was just going to walk into the kitchen, grasp my hand, and declare his undying love.

Based on past experiences with him, I had the very distinct feeling Bash would put up a wall and act as if nothing had happened. Or he'd use whatever emotions he was spiraling through to validate exactly why nothing should happen between us.

Bash was gone by the time I got out of the shower, but I refused to let it get me down. The night before had been freaking amazing and I wanted more, but I'd known from the moment he stepped into my room we'd need to cross some obstacles.

I stopped by Cravin'-a-Cup to see Leighton and pick up a morning jolt of caffeine.

"Why do you look like the cat who ate the canary?" Leighton asked, eyeing me up and down suspiciously.

Glancing at my phone, I realized I didn't have enough time to explain everything to Leighton, so I waved him off. "I'll tell you later."

My best friend pouted, but I couldn't help it. I needed to get to work so I could catch Bash before he barricaded himself behind his office door and hid from the world instead of facing the fact he'd let things between us go a lot further than he'd ever planned.

A few moments later, I had a large black coffee for

Bash, a steaming cup of butterfly pea flower tea for myself, and an iced chai latte for an afternoon treat.

Trying to decide if I should warn Bash I was coming or just barge in, I opted to text him just to be polite.

Me: I've got a coffee for you. Be there in about two minutes.

Bash: I'm busy. Thanks though.

Me: Figured you'd try that, but it won't work. We're going to talk about things. There's no use avoiding it.

Bash: I'd rather not. Let's just forget it happened.

Me: No can do. It happened. It happened spectacularly. We're going to acknowledge and discuss what it means for what's next.

Bash: Nothing. Nothing is next. We pretend nothing happened and move on.

IGNORING THAT LAST TEXT, I made my way to his office and knocked.

When Bash didn't answer, I situated my drinks and

tried the doorknob. Sticking my head around the door, I saw Bash, head in hands, hunched in a heap on his desk.

My heart went out to the guy, it really did.

Part of me felt bad because I knew he'd already had his life derailed and last night was one more thing that—in his mind—would be a disaster.

A tiny portion of my head wanted to be offended he was so distraught over hooking up with me and *maybe* seeing where things could go.

Like, was it *that* bad?

But the main part of me decided to just seize the day and make the best of what had happened.

"Hey," I said, placing the coffee cup on his desk. "Wasn't exactly sure what the standard gift is for when your boss walks in and catches you fucking yourself on a dildo suction-cupped to your headboard, tells you to keep going, and then joins in for the most spectacular spit roasting of your life." I tapped the top of the cup. "So, I went with the coffee, because last night? Ten of ten would recommend."

Bash groaned. "Oliver. Last night was a mistake I will regret forever. I was emotional from meeting with LuLu and I wasn't thinking. I should have *never* taken advantage of you in that way. I am so sorry."

I frowned, pushing away the sting of his words—I knew he was beating himself up, not trying to make me feel bad. "Are you kidding me right now? There was no taking advantage. Seriously, last night was easily in the number one spot of the entire existence of my sex life. I won't let you turn this into something you regret or ignore it and act like it never happened. It was good. *We* were good." I put my own drinks down and walked around his desk, perching my ass against the edge and placing a hand on his shoulder. "I think you can take a bit of time to process. Think through the fact LuLu is totally on board. Think about the fact it *is* kinda serendipitous we ended up in this situation in the first place—bonus points for Dad and LuLu knowing each other. Consider knowing what last night was like and never acting on it again—I don't know about you, but I'm not strong enough to experience that just once and never want the same and more again. Put aside your excuses, just let yourself feel." I dug my fingers into his shoulder. "I get that it's scary. I understand it's new and unplanned. But that doesn't mean it's bad or wrong." I tipped his chin and made him look at me. "I like you. I want to spend time with you. I want to see where this could go, which is about as weird as it gets for me because I've *never* wanted to take something further with a guy. Last night would have been a one-and-done, but that's not how I feel about this." I sighed, loving the rough stubble under my fingers. "Look, I'd never force you to do something you *truly* don't want to do, but I think you owe it to yourself—and me—to be honest about how you're feeling." I stood from the edge of his desk and retrieved my cups before moving toward the door. "I meant what I said about keeping everything professional at work. I'm going to get the day started. We can talk about this," I motioned between us, "at home. If you need me for anything work-related, give me a holler."

With that, I walked out of Bash's office and did everything I could to get my head screwed on straight for the day ahead.

———

My phone buzzed two hours later.

Bash: Can you come here, please?

My heart did a little happy dance, but we were at work so whatever he wanted me for was probably work related, and I'd promised to keep things professional.

I replied quickly I was finishing a small group and I'd be there in ten minutes.

When I popped my head into Bash's office, he gestured for me to enter and close the door.

"We have a problem," he said.

I wrinkled my nose. "Is it because I sucked you off last night and you're dying to have it happen again, but we have to wait until we're home?"

Bash made a strangled noise. "No, it's—"

"Are you worried LuLu likes me better and will want to adopt me? I think adopted brothers can still have sex. I bet there's a whole trope for shit like that."

"Damn it, Oliver," Bash growled.

I held up my hands. "Sorry, I'm nervous. I make jokes when I'm nervous."

Bash frowned. "Why are you nervous?"

I shrugged. "I don't know. What's wrong?"

He tossed a thick binder on the desk in front of him and motioned for me to sit down. "This is wrong. Ever since you mentioned the budget cuts I hadn't been told about, I've been digging through the books. There are a lot of discrepancies."

"No, Elise was good. She wouldn't have done anything wrong," I said, feeling defensive of my old director.

"What did you really know about her?" Bash asked. "Did you know her personally or did you just like her because she was personable, mostly left you alone, and let you run things the way you wanted?"

I started to protest, but realized his words were accurate. Deflating, I slumped back against the chair. "Okay, pretty much the latter. But that doesn't mean she did anything wrong. What kind of discrepancies are you seeing?"

"I've gone over things multiple times and there are big chunks of money missing over several years. Most of it is in small amounts here and there, but there are some bigger amounts missing in a few spots—usually hidden between large purchases for the center."

"So, Elise was stealing from the center?" I shook my head. "I just can't picture that."

"Did someone else do the books?"

"No, the director is in charge of that. But wouldn't things have shown up in our taxes?"

Bash shrugged. "I thought of that. Do you think the accountant was in on it?"

I took a deep breath. "Shit, I don't know. That's all beyond me. I didn't have anything to do with the money, none of us did besides the director. Elise answered to the owner, Mr. Eller, but he was getting older and she always talked about how she did a lot to take things off his plate."

I rolled my eyes. "And by taking things off his plate, she was able to hide what she was doing. Shit."

"I'm also confused why she left things in plain sight. These books were just in a filing cabinet for anyone to look at. Makes me wonder what Elise had planned if she didn't think she needed to hide the books." Bash absently flipped through a couple pages. "Did she leave abruptly? Or did the staff know she'd been planning to leave?"

"It was fast. Like, one day she was here, the next day she was gone." I remembered being shocked to find out we were without a director, but Mr. Eller had assured us he would find a suitable replacement.

"Have you heard from her since?" Bash asked.

"Not a peep. Seemed weird, but like you said, we basically only knew her in a professional setting. I've got phone numbers for some of my colleagues, but not all of them. Elise had access to staff contact information, but we didn't have hers."

Bash scowled. "What if you needed to call in sick? Or had an emergency?"

I shrugged. "Elise wasn't like that. We were to call the front desk and leave a message in addition to emailing her center account. Doctor notes or funeral programs, shit like that, all went through the front desk. Elise was friendly enough, but she stayed to herself—she wasn't out and about like you are. After the first year of working here, she worked two or three days a week from home." Realization washed over me as I thought about just how distant and unknown our boss had been. "Most meetings were done virtually. She didn't do much face-to-face with the parents, preferring to communicate through email if the department head couldn't take care of an issue. She said it was for a paper trail, but thinking back on all of it now, I'm wondering if it was because she was a thief. Maybe she kept herself apart and distant so no one could start digging?" I shook my head, feeling like a fool. "Damn. She was good at it. Who knew I was so blind to a crime happening right under my nose as long as the perpetrator left me alone to run my department the way I thought was best?"

"It wasn't just you. If Elise was doing what I think she was doing, she had everybody wearing blinders. The missing money is evident—anyone with half a brain could see it if they took a look at these books—but the part I can't figure out is why she just up and left. If she'd been fired, I'd think she would have found a way to get the financial records out of the office to keep her name clear. She had to know someone would eventually take over for her and start looking—especially when she didn't even hide what she was doing."

"I don't think she was fired. When Mr. Eller told us she was no longer the director, he just said she'd called him the night before and let him know she regretted to inform him she wouldn't be returning due to personal reasons."

Bash's eyes met mine. "That's suspicious."

"Thinking about it now, yeah. Mr. Eller has been a bit more out of touch in the last year or so, I'm guessing he didn't even question it." I clenched my fist. "Fuck her for stealing from him and this place. We work hard and we do a lot of good, what kind of piece of shit steals from a place that helps kids?"

"Yeah, it's a big mess."

"What can we do about it?" I asked, ready to fight tooth and nail for the workplace I loved.

"Well, that's the other issue." Bash grimaced.

"You're just full of good news today," I deadpanned. "What?"

"We've got a new owner. Mr. Eller has handed the reins to his daughter, Danica. She called about an hour ago and let me know she's coming for a visit. She didn't come straight out and say it, but she indicated she had some concerns. Said she's hopeful to make the transition as easy as possible, didn't sound like she planned to make huge changes. But I have to let her know what I've found, if she hasn't already discovered it."

"If you found the holes so easily, she probably could too, right?"

Bash nodded. "If she's looked into anything, even if she wasn't looking for something wrong, she likely could have found it. She needs to know about the accountant— that person was either in on it or willing to turn a blind eye."

"At least you're safe, you've not been here long enough to be the one stealing money. Danica won't think it's you."

"True, but I need to make sure she's aware of all of this. It can't look like I found the problem and sat on it."

"What do you need from me?" A trickle of warmth wiggled through me. The fact Bash called me in and told me what was happening meant...well, I wasn't sure, but it meant something. "I'll help in any way I can."

"Danica asked for you by name. She'd been looking at

the staff roster, noticed you'd been here the longest I guess. She's coming first of next week and I told her we could meet with her." Bash tapped his fingers on the desk. "Are you able to clear your day so we're available for her?"

"Not a problem. What else do you need from me?"

Bash sighed. "I think we just wait to see what Danica brings to us and go from there."

"Sounds good. And we'll recharge this weekend to be ready for her. No work talk at home," I said as I stood from my chair. "The only thing you and I are talking about at home is…" I pointed back and forth between us with a grin.

Bash groaned. "You're not going to just accept my apology and move on?"

"Are you kidding me? First, *stop* apologizing—it couldn't have been *that* bad. Second, please just have an open mind." I crossed my arms over my chest. "In fact, if you don't agree to at least give some thought to the two of us becoming an actual *us*—and I promise I'm not angling for a ring or happily ever after—" Although, for the first time in my adult life I wasn't scared shitless of the thought. "But if you don't at least give it some thought, I'm going to tell LuLu what happened last night—how much detail I go into depends on how stubborn you're being—and see what she thinks."

Bash's face drained of color. "You wouldn't."

"Try me. You can't say last night wasn't good. You can't say you aren't dying for more of the same. You're lying if you do."

Now it was his turn to cross his arms over his chest. "Whether it was good or not—"

I scoffed. "Don't even act like it wasn't the hottest night of sex you've ever had."

Bash pinched the bridge of his nose. "None of that has anything to do with the fact you're so much younger than me and we work together."

"Colleagues fuck. Bosses and employees fuck. Let's be realistic. That's a terrible excuse. Almost as bad as the age one. Who. The. Fuck. Cares. About our age difference? You. Just you." I walked around his desk and stepped close enough I could smell his unique lemon, sage, and leather scent. "Tell me right now you don't find me attractive."

Bash closed his eyes.

"That's what I thought." I brushed the back of my finger down his arm. "Tell me right now a single valid reason our ages have anything to do with us falling into bed or going out on a date."

He swallowed, his Adam's apple bobbing. "People will look at us. Think I'm your dad."

"Again, who cares? People already look at you because you're hot as sin. I'll be sure to be just obnoxiously over-the-top enough with hand holding and kisses most wouldn't even think I'm your son—plus, we look *nothing* alike. Those excuses have been shot down." My pinky pressed against his, my heart soaring when Bash moved his finger to lay on top of mine. "Your aunt loves me. We get along. Just give in and let it happen."

Bash cleared his throat and stepped back. "We'll see. I just don't know if it's the best idea."

"Or you know it's the best idea and you're just not sure what to do with it." I stepped back into his space and leaned in to whisper, "That's okay. It's not like you can escape me. If we're not together at work, you'll find me at home—either in the kitchen, the living room, or fucking myself on a dildo attached to my headboard dreaming of it being you pounding into me."

Bash made a strangled choking noise as I grinned and walked out of his office.

Keeping things strictly professional at work was a much bigger challenge than I'd originally anticipated.

———

"WHAT DO you want to do for your birthday?" Julian put his arm around me while the eight of us were gathered in and around the kitchen Thursday morning—eating, packing lunches, and sipping coffee, or in my case, chocolate milk.

It was so rare to have us all in one place at one time, I couldn't help the buzz of happiness in my veins.

"Something fun," I answered at the exact same moment as Bash turned confused eyes toward my brother and answered, "Nothing really. Birthdays aren't my thing."

Julian glanced between Bash and me, smiling smugly as if he knew something we didn't.

"Sorry," Bash said quickly. "I thought...never mind. When is your birthday?"

I cocked my head and gave a quick narrow-eyed look to my brother before answering, "Sunday. Why, when is yours?"

Bash's eyes went wide and he hesitated.

"Well, as the apartment manager privy to resident information, I wouldn't be able to divulge that type of information even if I noticed it right away." Julian chuckled softly, keeping me tucked against him. "Bash, your birthday is…" he let the question trail off as Bash rolled his eyes.

"My birthday is Sunday," Bash said in a voice that told me just how much he hated admitting it.

"Oh my god," Leighton squealed so loudly Jett winced and clapped a hand over his mouth. Leighton must have licked Jett's palm because he jerked his hand away with a grunt. "Bash and Ollie have the same birthday? That's like the cutest, most meant to be thing in the world! Work together, room together, celebrate together—it's like you were put on this earth to find each other. You *have* to kiss and do butt stuff and fall in love." Leighton clasped his hands together and sighed. "I love love."

"Gotta say, that's pretty cool," Lucas said. "You two already had a bit of fate or whatever going on, but you share a birthday? Almost like you can't deny it now."

I caught Bash's eye and didn't miss the pink in his cheeks, but I wasn't going to put him on the spot right then. "So, I want to go ride roller coasters. Please tell me we can all get time off, at least sometime in the next six months."

"Dean and I have the weekend off," Shaw offered softly.

"I actually switched shifts with someone, so I'm off too," Lucas said.

Julian shrugged. "I can have Chloe cover for the weekend. Leighton? Jett?"

"Let me see if I can juggle a couple appointments," Jett said.

Leighton beamed. "I can definitely switch a shift." He turned toward Bash and me. "You two don't work most weekends, right? So, you're free?"

The thought of all eight of us being able to go somewhere as a group had me floating on cloud nine. It was strange how quickly we'd all gelled so easily—aside from my dad, I definitely considered this group of men my closest friends.

"We're free. Can we leave tomorrow after work? Everyone good with that? I'll get a van rented," I offered. "We'll need a room, right?"

"I'll do the park tickets and you can all pay me—Bash and Ollie, your tickets and room are on us," Dean said.

"Let me rent the van," Julian said. "I can get a discount I think."

"I'll call about a room," Lucas said.

Bash cleared his throat. "Sorry, but what's happening here?"

"We're all going to Wild Ride for our birthday," I said, nudging my shoulder against his. "Fun, right?"

"If by fun you mean something that sounds like a nightmare, sure." Bash shook his head. "You all go and have fun, it's just not my scene."

"Have you ever been to Wild Ride?" Leighton asked.

"No, but—"

"Then you don't know it's not your scene," Leighton interrupted. "Come on, if you don't go, it will be like tempting fate. You guys share a birthday. Plus, without you, we'll have an odd number and someone will have to ride by themselves."

"I don't have to go," Shaw piped up. "If it's easier to just have six instead of eight."

"No way, you're going," Julian said and shot a glare toward Bash. "The fact all eight of us can go so easily means we should definitely take advantage of it. We could all use a weekend away."

Bash pursed his lips at Julian's insistence, but nodded begrudgingly. "Fine. I'll go." He looked my way. "So much for recharging this weekend before our meeting."

I shook my head. "No, this will be great. The thrill of riding roller coasters, amusement park food, road trip with the guys, nothing better to get us ready for our meeting."

Between the sexual encounter I'd shared with Bash, finding out we had the same birthday, and scoring the rarest of rare weekends away with *all* my roommates, I was absolutely soaring.

And I definitely had a bit of a fantasy building in my head about spending the weekend with Bash on our little road trip.

Leighton would be glued to Jett's side.

Dean and Lucas were a bestie package deal.

Julian hardly ever took his eyes off Shaw.

So that left Bash and me to partner up.

I smiled as we headed off to work.

Partner up with Bash? Don't mind if I do.

I think I grinned the entire day.

EIGHT

Bash
___

WHY?

Why was this happening?

Why did I have roommates who liked to go to amusement parks?

Why did I agree to go to said amusement park?

I sighed as I stared at my closet on Friday afternoon.

I needed to pack for a road trip I didn't really want to go on.

Well, honestly, it wasn't the road trip I was against. I just wasn't sure about Wild Ride. I'd never actually been to an amusement park or ridden on a roller coaster.

Yes, I realized how pathetic that sounded as a forty-two-year-old man, but it was what it was.

LuLu used to take me places, but it was usually renaissance fairs or health conferences or Broadway shows. Thinking back on it, I was actually surprised she didn't take me to an amusement park—she was definitely a thrill seeker. But I guess the hikes, skiing, and bungee jumping we did made up for the lack of roller coasters.

Between the financial issue at work, a new director, the unknown of the weekend, and whatever was happening between Ollie and me, my head felt as if it was about to explode.

The weekend and Ollie were top of my overwhelming list.

No matter how badly I wanted to pretend like it was nothing, there was definitely something happening between Ollie and me.

But before I could think about that, I needed to get a handle on this road trip.

First, what did one wear to an amusement park?

Second, I knew without a doubt I'd be partnered up with Ollie. That was a given.

How in the world could I dread being paired with him while simultaneously looking so forward to it?

Probably the same way I could be so full of guilt and regret at what I let happen when I walked in on him, while still being so damn turned on and dying to do it again, I could hardly think straight.

I was fucked.

So. Very. Fucked.

How would it look if Ollie and I were to become a thing?

Like I was going through a midlife crisis and trying to reclaim my youth by fucking around with a guy half my age.

Ollie was right. I shouldn't care. But I worried all the same.

Play the part, look the part—the right clothes, the

right job, the right relationship. If those things were all in place, no one would see or care about the rest being in shambles. That way of thinking had come from my parents. Even after Mom died and Dad gave up on me, that mindset stuck around. LuLu had done what she could to shape my thinking differently—and she'd helped a lot— but I still had issues with how people saw me and thought of me.

As long as I could portray the right façade, it didn't matter what my reality was like—or that was what I told myself.

As badly as I wanted to throw caution to the wind and see what could happen between Ollie and me, there was still a large part of me worried about how it would look, how it might affect my job, how it might derail my plans.

Although, to be honest, I hadn't given much thought to those future plans since coming to Cravenwood Block.

Resting my forehead against the closet door frame, I let my thoughts drift back to the night I'd walked in on Ollie. For the millionth time, I relived the moment I noticed his door was cracked and the sounds coming from within.

Why hadn't I just walked away?

So fucking stupid.

But from the second I'd caught sight of him spread open, thrusting his ass onto that dildo, I'd lost all hope of making good decisions.

I wanted to swallow each and every little whimper and moan he made.

Wanted to hold him, touch him, taste him, fuck him.

Dear god, how I wanted those things.

And for that one moment, suspended in time, Ollie was begging for the same.

So, I gave in.

And it was spectacular.

Watching him get off, the heat of his mouth on me, coming like I'd never come before.

But the guilt had crashed hard.

Despite how Ollie had pleaded with me to join him.

No matter how good it had felt.

I regretted it.

No, actually, I only regretted it was over so quickly and I hadn't been able to kiss him and hold him.

Damn, man, you're an idiot. If you walked into his room right now, you know good and well Ollie would drop everything to have you kiss him and hold him.

I did know that.

And I wanted it so badly.

But the situation in his bedroom was still a one-time deal and could be written off as stupidity and ignored—or so I kept telling myself.

If I allowed something else to happen—if I admitted I wanted something else to happen—then I had to deal with the possibility of dating and feelings and more.

I didn't want to hurt Ollie.

Hell, I didn't want to hurt myself. I was already more emotionally involved with Ollie than I'd ever been with Randal. The thing with Randal had looked good, had been the perfect part to play, but it hadn't been real.

Not that I really knew what *real* was, but the feelings I had for Ollie were heady and all-consuming. I didn't know how to handle them. Didn't know what to do with them. Didn't know what they meant for now or the future.

Yeah, I was very likely overthinking things.

Ollie probably just wanted to fuck and move on.

Don't dismiss him like that. He's been upfront and open about wanting to date and feeling differently toward you than any other guy.

It actually would have been easier—maybe?—if Ollie had just wanted to fuck around a few times and then move on.

Living and working together would have made that awkward, but at least it would have been quick and easy.

But those gorgeous deep brown eyes were full of desire, mischief, and hope when he talked about us dating. I believed him when he said he wasn't looking for forever, but I wasn't sure how to handle the little niggle in my heart that said maybe I was.

I heard commotion in the kitchen and realized I'd zoned out instead of packing.

I threw on a pair of khakis and a polo, packing a pair of jeans and another polo just as Leighton peeked his head into my room.

"Hey you about ready…oh god, no. Sweet baby Jesus, you poor child." He sashayed into the room and grabbed my elbow, looking me up and down. "We're leaving soon. For a road trip and roller coaster riding. What in the name of gay boys everywhere are you wearing?"

"You said casual," I defended.

"Casual. Like *casual*," he said, gesturing to his shorts and tank. "Not business casual."

I winced. "I don't have anything like that."

"What about workout clothes?"

Shaking my head, I plopped onto my bed. "In storage. Can I just not go?"

"Don't even talk that way. This trip is bestie-building at its best. Plus, it's a birthday party. No worries. Give me five minutes and I'll be back." He picked up my bag and took out the jeans and polo. "Your assignment is to pack toiletries and such. Do you have tennis shoes, like the kind that would be good for walking?"

I nodded. "Yeah, I grabbed those, just not my workout clothes." I'd been telling myself I needed to go get my gym clothes, but hadn't made it there yet. Swimming and sitting in the sauna had become my workout and destressing activity of choice lately.

Leighton disappeared and I set to work packing sunscreen, toothbrush, deodorant, charger, and other needed items.

When he returned, Leighton had an arm full of clothes.

"Okay, this is for the ride over," he said, tossing what looked to be joggers and a t-shirt at me. "You can wear those on the ride back, too. This is for the park." He threw a pair of mesh basketball shorts and a t-shirt on the bed. "I highly suggest a pair of well-fitting boxer briefs to reduce chafing. It will be warm and we'll be walking a lot." He glanced at his phone. "Come on, change your clothes. We're leaving soon."

Thirty minutes later, the eight of us were piled into a rented 12-passenger van. Julian punched in the address to Wild Ride and we headed off. The plan was to stop for a quick dinner, arrive at our hotel by ten o'clock, get a decent night's sleep, and hit the park when they opened on Saturday morning. We'd stay until closing, sleep at the hotel, and drive back Sunday morning.

As I'd figured, Ollie and I were already partnered up. Julian was driving and Shaw was in the front seat with him. Lucas and Dean were on the smaller middle bench seat. Leighton and Jett sat next to Ollie and me on the longer back bench seat. It was a pretty comfortable ride, and I couldn't say it bothered me at all to have Ollie pressed against me.

The conversation flowed easily as we headed toward our destination—a comfortable togetherness settling over the vehicle. Aside from time with LuLu, I'd never felt so *right* with a group of people.

Yes, a lot of it was because the men surrounding me were just good guys, but—as much as I hated to admit it —a large part of it was because of the man seated next to me.

As we unloaded at the restaurant about ninety minutes into our drive, Julian called out, "Bash, can you take a look at this?"

Everyone gave him a strange look—me included— wondering what in the world he'd need me to look at, but they headed inside and I hung back with Julian.

"What's up?" I asked, suddenly feeling like I was on trial.

"Just wanted to say thanks for coming on this trip. Shaw needs this time away and the chance to make some friends, but he would have totally stayed home if he'd thought he was going to be the odd man out." Julian clapped me on the shoulder.

"Oh, yeah, sure. Not a problem. The speed this trip got planned—and the destination—kinda threw me for a loop, but I don't mind taking the weekend, especially with the week we've got coming up." I shrugged. "Can't say I have experience with it, but I'm sure we'll have fun."

"Not a fan of roller coasters?" Julian asked with a grin.

"Don't know. Never been on one."

A look of surprise crossed his face. "Well, Ollie *loves* them. He'll take care of you."

Desire and guilt flooded through me as I thought of how well Ollie had *taken care of me* a few nights ago.

Julian chuckled. "Pretty sure I don't want to know what my little brother did to cause that look." He shook his head. "Look, I know Ollie can come on strong, but he's a really good guy—has a great heart. It's not really my place to spill his secrets, but let's just say there's a lot in his past that made him the type of person who jokes and says outlandish things."

I glanced toward the doors Ollie had walked through. "If I had to guess, he's like that because he learned at an early age it was an easy way to hide the fear and pain of what life with his mom and her men was like."

"Something like that, yeah." Julian's face showed compassion for his brother as he pocketed the keys. "So, I was thinking...no one can force two people to like each other—and I'd never think of doing that if I didn't think you and Ollie already had a sort of connection. I guess I'm just saying maybe use this weekend as a chance to get to know him better."

I frowned. "I don't want to lead him on."

"It's only leading him on if you have no interest whatsoever. Can you say that?" Julian asked quietly.

I sighed. "No."

"Then maybe let this weekend be a time to let down your guard. Let Ollie be himself, you be yourself, and see where it takes you." Julian chuckled. "I'm not saying fuck him in our hotel room, but don't work so hard to keep the walls up."

"I hear what you're saying," was all I could offer. "I just don't want him to get his hopes up and then have me end up not able to follow through."

"I get that. I'm not suggesting declarations of love, just maybe be open to his flirting? Ollie's going to flirt—it's who he is. Might as well enjoy it."

We headed into the restaurant to meet our friends. Dinner was a happy, boisterous affair. I barely had time to think about what Julian had said because I was so busy laughing with the guys.

A few times during dinner, I caught looks between the other guys and I wondered if any of them recognized how smitten they were.

Jett looked at Leighton like he was sunshine on a cloudy day.

Shaw was clearly in awe of Julian and the feeling was definitely mutual even if neither of them had addressed it —and maybe never would. Honestly, if someone saw them together, they'd for sure think Julian and Shaw were a couple based on the slight touches and googly eyes.

Lucas and Dean were the most interesting. From what I had gathered, the two had grown up together as best friends. Lucas had come out as bisexual sometime around late high school or early college. Dean claimed to be straight and dated women. Lucas dated women from time-to-time, but didn't shy away from men either.

They both were clearly jealous when the other dated. They looked at each other with stars in their eyes and like they wanted to eat each other alive.

They never dated anyone for long and the people they dated always took a back seat to the relationship between Lucas and Dean.

I wondered if they'd ever figure out they were completely and totally in love with each other. Every so often, I got the feeling Lucas maybe already recognized his feelings for Dean, but I wasn't sure he would ever act on it —unless he ever got a signal from Dean.

As we loaded back into the van after dinner, Ollie stated he'd be taking song requests for the rest of our drive. The van was filled with music, mediocre singing, and laughter for the next two hours.

Bash of the past would have been appalled, but it amazed me how having the right people around could totally change the outlook on a situation.

"I thought we got a hotel," Julian said as he pulled up to an apartment complex type location.

"No, I said I'd call about a room," Lucas said. "I went the AirBnB route. The one I got has two bathrooms and sleeps eight. We're really only here to sleep, right? Figured we didn't need anything fancy."

No one could really argue with the logic, and the building looked to be clean and well-kept in a decent part of town.

"It's close to the park, too. We'll be able to head out early, grab breakfast, and be in line before the gates open," Dean added.

We unloaded the van as Lucas fiddled with the key code on the door.

Before long, the eight of us were standing in the middle of a creatively renovated apartment. The owners had obviously taken advantage of the AirBnB mindset and their close proximity to the amusement park when they remodeled the apartment.

"From the listing, it seems like they've got other units on property that sleep only two to four people, and I thought about getting two of those," Lucas explained. "But this one could fit us all and it was dirt cheap due to a last-minute cancellation."

The lodging had clearly once been two separate studio apartments, but the shared wall had been cut out and replaced with an interesting archway between the two. Four king-sized beds took up most of the space in both halves of the apartment, with only a desk, dresser, bedside table, and two floor lamps squeezed in on each side of the shared arch.

"I call dibs on a shower," Leighton crowed, tossing his bag onto one of the beds. He twirled his way over to Jett and whispered something in his ear that had Jett's cheeks turning pink.

Jett dropped his own bag on the same bed and let himself be pulled toward the bathroom as Leighton sing-songed something about saving water and protecting the planet.

Lucas tackled Dean onto one of the other beds and the four of us remaining watched them wrestle around.

"Do you think they'll ever admit it?" Shaw asked quietly.

"Eventually, yeah," Julian said. "One of them is going to finally be hit smack dab in the face with the realization —I just hope it's before either of them has settled down."

Ollie snorted. "There's no way they're settling unless it's with each other. They are attached at the hip—connected heart-to-heart with an invisible tether. Yeah, I think they'll eventually see what's right in front of them."

"Um," Shaw said tentatively as he pulled his gaze from Lucas and Dean and glanced between the two remaining beds. "I can sleep on the floor…"

"No one is sleeping on the floor," Julian said.

For the first time since walking into our overnight accommodations, I realized I'd inadvertently been trapped in a slightly altered *there's only one bed* situation.

Fuck.

Ollie tossed his bag next to one bed and flopped down, folding his arms behind his head and grinning at me like a damn hungry Cheshire cat ready to claim his prize.

Julian looked at me as if he'd wring my neck if I dared take away his chance to sleep with Shaw.

Shaw's eyes held a glowing trepidation—whether because of the mere thought of sleeping with Julian or fear of having to share a bed with Ollie or me.

I wasn't going to mess things up for Shaw, and I had no desire to be strangled by Julian, so I pulled up my big boy undies and placed my bag next to Ollie's bed. The mattress was gigantic, we'd have a mile of space between us, and it was only for a couple nights.

"Promise I won't maul you," Ollie teased with a waggle of his brow. "Unless you ask nicely."

Lucas finally gave up on wrestling Dean and went to the bathroom door. "Saving water only counts if you don't take a double-long shower. Other people want to get clean, hurry up. And use shower spray when you're done, no one wants to shower with the remnants of your jizz!" he hollered through the door.

He turned and pointed a finger between Ollie and me. "That goes for the two of you as well. If you're getting off in the shower, clean up after."

Ollie snorted. "I will, if you will. Pretty sure both showers at home have had more than their fair share of loads shot onto the walls and tricking down the drains."

I shot up from the bed and riffled through my bag, doing everything in my power to avoid thinking about Ollie getting himself off in our shower. "I'll be quick. Just wanna wash off and head to bed," I mumbled as I headed toward the second bathroom with a pair of boxers and my toothbrush in hand.

After a quick, *cold* shower where I refused to let my mind wander—only keeping myself from jerking off to the image of a hard, wet Ollie because my seven roommates were right on the other side of the door—I brushed my teeth, toweled my hair dry, and pulled on my boxers.

All of us had quickly grown accustomed to being in various states of undress around each other. Lucas and Leighton were most likely to be in just underwear—sometimes full-coverage, but often very skimpy.

Ollie, Jett, Dean, Julian, and I were usually in boxers or boxer briefs, often times throwing on a tank or t-shirt if we were going to be around the group for more than just a trip to the kitchen.

Shaw was the most modest and almost always wore lounge pants and a shirt even if just making a run to the fridge or microwave from his room.

I made my way to the bed where Ollie's eyes devoured my boxers-only clad body.

It's just a couple nights. No big deal.

Leighton and Jett emerged from whatever fun they'd been having and immediately crawled into bed.

"No fornicating while we're all here to witness it," Lucas warned.

"It's bad enough we have to hear it," Julian added. "Just don't make us see it."

Leighton giggled and Jett shot us the bird.

Over the next hour, everyone showered and settled into their beds, charging phones, setting alarms, and preparing for the next day.

Despite the new bed, and having Ollie sharing it with me, the exhaustion from working all day and the long drive caught up with me. Ignoring the strong desire to pull Ollie close, to feel his warmth, to bury my face in his neck and breathe in his sweet strawberries and mint scent, I rolled to my side to face away from him.

My plan was to be up earlier than anyone else so I could get ready and maybe go grab coffee from the gas station about a block down. That way, I'd be out of everyone's way and able to separate myself from the Ollie-related feelings churning in my gut.

Praying the distance between us would be enough to make it through the night—knowing I was a cuddler if given the chance—I made a final check of my alarm and settled in to sleep.

It took a moment to remember where I was when I woke, but the hushed voices around me were a quick reminder. I kept my eyes closed and listened.

"Nah, let them sleep for a little longer," Lucas whispered. "You know this is like Ollie's dream come true."

"Not sure Bash would complain either—if he's being honest," Jett said.

"I think it's sweet," Leighton said. "They look good together, right?"

A throat cleared. "If anyone needs to shower, go ahead," Julian said. "Shaw, you wanna walk with me to get coffee?"

The front door opened and closed.

Damn it.

My alarm hadn't gone off.

And I was wrapped around a snuggly warm Ollie.

On display for everyone to see.

Our legs were tangled.

My hand over his where his arms were tucked against his chest.

He smelled so damn good.

In a fantasy world, I'd angle his head toward mine and gently kiss him awake. Kiss him the way I'd missed out on during our encounter the other night. Lick his lips open, savor the taste of him on my tongue.

Why can't your fantasy be reality?

I rolled my eyes at the ridiculous thought. First, we had an audience. I wasn't against public displays of affection, but Ollie and I weren't an actual couple—even though the whole crew seemed to think we'd at least be playing one for the weekend.

Second, I wasn't sure I'd want to stop at kissing.

And that morning wasn't the time to puzzle through what I was feeling with Ollie cuddled in my arms. I desperately needed to move my thoughts elsewhere.

The sounds in the apartment told me the guys were getting ready for the day. Jett and Leighton laughing and whispering in one bathroom, Lucas and Dean joking around while pulling on clothes.

I felt the moment Ollie woke up. He came awake slowly, making to roll over, and froze. Grateful he hadn't moved to face me—if our morning wood met up, I wasn't sure I'd be able to leave the bed—I waited to see how he would react to being tangled in my arms.

"Pretty sure I could get used to waking up like this every morning," he murmured, stretching and yawning.

Fuck. You and me both.

Ollie patted my hand and spoke softly. "But I'm sure this is freaking you out a bit, so I'll tuck the moment away for relishing at a different time, and we can get up and get ready. We've got a whole day of fun ahead of us. Can we please not be weird about this?"

I chuckled into his hair, not wanting to let him go. "Sorry, I'm a sleep cuddler. Always have been; used to have about twenty stuffed animals to snuggle with when I was a kid. Not going to be weird, promise." Fighting the urge to kiss his neck or ear or anywhere my lips could find skin, I said, "If I'm weird at all, it's because I've never been on a roller coaster. Not gonna lie, I'm a bit nervous."

We disentangled ourselves as Ollie spoke. "Are you afraid of heights?"

"No, I've been bungee jumping and loved it. LuLu took me a lot of places for fun, but we somehow never made it to roller coasters."

"Then it's all good. The coasters are a lot of fun." Ollie leaned close, his lips near my ear, the snuggly scent of sleep like a cloud around us. "I liked waking up with you," he whispered. "Now come on, chop chop." He laughed when I yelped at the smack he landed on my ass.

We were up and out of the apartment with an hour and a half before the park opened. Our hope was to eat at a diner we'd seen when we drove in and get to the park to be in line when the gates opened.

"If we're a bit past that time, it's all good," Lucas said. "Dean will make us all pause to put on sunscreen before we go in anyway."

Dean rolled his eyes. "Sorry, but I'd prefer we not get skin cancer. Plus, I don't want to hear the complaining that would come from sunburns."

"Ollie, Leighton, and I probably need extra layers slathered on," Lucas said, batting his lashes. "We're so fair and fragile."

"I definitely burn easily," Ollie said. "Bring on the SPF."

"Do you have to make sure your tattoos are protected?" I asked Jett.

He nodded. "Yeah, the sun can really fuck with the colors, fades things out for sure."

We pulled in at the diner and Julian found a spot where the van could fit before we piled out and headed inside.

Delicious scents of bacon, syrup, and coffee bombarded us as we opened the door. The air was icy cold and excited anticipation hung in the air as groups of park-goers ate their breakfast and talked about their plans for the day.

We opted to squeeze into one big round corner booth rather than splitting between two tables. In the past, I would have been bent out of shape over it, arguing it would make more sense to just use two tables, but with the happiness on my friends' faces and Ollie's thigh pressed against mine, I didn't really have it in me to argue the tight quarters.

"LuLu and I used to stop at little roadside diners when we'd travel. She never wanted to hit chain restaurants, always looked for out-of-the-way local places to give her money to," I told Ollie after we'd all placed our orders.

"I can see that. I bet she was fun to travel with," Ollie said.

I smiled. "She was. Still is, actually. She maybe wouldn't be up for roller coasters these days—although, with her, you never know—but she likes to hike."

"I'm not a huge nature lover, but we should take her hiking sometime. If she's going to be my new grandma, we should spend time together."

I huffed out a laugh and rolled my eyes. "She'd like

that," I said, unsure of what to do with the feelings roiling through me—feelings about sharing Ollie and LuLu, feelings about Ollie becoming *more* in my life—feelings of confusion, simmering anticipation, and uncertainty.

Ollie bumped my shoulder and grinned, tearing me away from the thoughts as if he knew I'd ventured way too far into serious thinking on a fun weekend.

The food was delicious and we all grumbled about needing a nap as we paid and loaded back into the van. Julian expertly maneuvered the van through traffic and got us to the park with thirty minutes before the gates opened.

Of course, everyone and their brother had pretty much had the same idea, but Lucas and Ollie insisted we had all day and didn't need to get worked up over lines.

"Remember, this is a celebration trip," Lucas said. "And we're destressing, not *distressing*. We're here to have fun."

Ollie, Lucas, Leighton, and Julian donned backpacks and the other four of us helped stock them with water bottles, phone chargers, sunscreen, Tylenol, bandaids, and lip balms. The plan was one backpack per partner pair and we'd share the load of carrying it around.

"Toss your wallets in the bags if you want, safer than having them banging around in your pocket and falling out on a ride," Lucas advised.

"Okay, time for sunscreen," Dean said, handing everyone a spray can of SPF 50.

"You do me and I'll do you," Ollie teased, waggling his brow.

We spent the next several moments, tucked under a shade tree in the parking lot, spraying sunscreen over exposed skin, rubbing it in, and applying a face stick to cheeks, foreheads, ears, and noses. It reminded me of LuLu slathering me up before we'd go hiking way back then.

When we finally made it into line, we only had about ten minutes to wait. The day wasn't yet too hot and a cool breeze danced over my sunscreen-clammy skin.

Jett and Leighton were the obvious couple in our group. Holding hands, sharing smiles, anyone could tell they were together.

Lucas and Dean hung together like best friends, and only if you'd known them for a while would you notice the occasional look of longing on Lucas's face. Dean maybe hadn't recognized the feelings in himself yet, but the two of them definitely had secret smiles and the powerful connection of a shared past.

Julian and Shaw were adorable. Julian seemed to find himself putting a protective arm around Shaw quite often, and Shaw looked as if he wanted to curl into Julian's side and never leave. The tension and attraction between them were thick. I wanted to push them together and give them both some relief, but it definitely wasn't my place.

I wondered what folks saw when they looked at Ollie and me. Standing in line, walking toward our next ride, stopping under a shade tree to hydrate or reapply sunscreen throughout the day, did Ollie and I appear *together* because the others were partnered up? Or was there a *something more* quality others saw?

The roller coasters turned out to be a lot of fun and I

wished LuLu and I had experienced the thrill of riding back when she was younger. She would have loved the breathless excitement of the monstrous rides.

The eight of us mostly stuck together throughout the day, standing in line together—sharing chit-chat and laughs—waiting for each other at the end of rides, hanging together as we discussed which ride we'd get on next. At one of our many breaks for food—come on, we were on a mini vacation at an amusement park, of course we'd eat all the junk—Ollie, Leighton, and Shaw took off together to check out a shop while Jett, Lucas, and Dean went to order food and drinks.

Julian and I secured a table in the shade in a quieter area of the park while waiting for the guys to return.

"Don't like being thought of as old," Julian said, "but I'm not gonna complain about being the ones to hold the table. My feet are ready for the break."

I laughed. "Agreed."

My gaze drifted to the shop across the way where Ollie and his friends had gone to search for souvenirs.

"Does the age thing bother you?" I asked.

Julian cocked a brow.

"You're what? Thirty-five? Shaw's like twenty-three?"

"Twenty-four," Julian answered absently.

"Is it an issue for you?"

Julian frowned. "We're friends and roommates, age doesn't matter."

I studied him for a moment. "Ohhh, so that's the way you're playing it? You can assume things about Ollie and me, encourage it, play the protective big brother, but when it comes to admitting you've got a thing for Shaw, that's off limits? Gotcha." I smirked and rolled my eyes.

Julian huffed. "I don't know that Shaw is ready for anything between us. He's got a lot in his past and I think he needs a friend more than anything right now."

"If there was ever more between you, would the age thing bother you?" I pressed.

Julian shrugged. "Maybe. I think I'd mostly worry it would look like me taking advantage of a younger guy with a lot of hurts. Not that I'd do that or Shaw is some weakling to be taken advantage of—I think I'd just worry that's what it might *look* like."

"Do you think I'd be taking advantage of Ollie if we explored things between us?"

"Not at all. Ollie is strong. If he didn't want anything to do with you, you'd know it and wouldn't be able to get close to him. He's young, but he's got a good head on his shoulders. He maybe doesn't have a lot of experience with dating or love," he broke off and held up his hands to placate my immediate protests over the L-word, "but he's smart and independent, he knows what he wants and doesn't want." Julian chuckled. "And he wants you."

"To what end?"

Julian glanced toward where the shopping trio was making their way out of the store. "In the past? I'd say a couple weeks of fun. Now? With you? He's different. I can't say for sure how long or to what degree—that's between the two of you, and really, none of us know how long something is going to last, even if we want forever— but I don't think he's angling for just a fling." He paused, flicking a leaf from the table. "What about you? What do you want?"

Sighing, I shook my head. "Until Ollie, I thought I didn't want anything to do with relationships ever again. I was going to use this job as a reset before moving on to bigger and better, wasn't going to get attached to Cravenwood. I had my aunt to worry about, but I didn't want to get involved with anything outside of building my resume and finding a good job with a stable future."

"Now?"

I gestured toward the three men approaching. "Ollie shoved his way into my life and threw everything off course." The words sounded fond even to my ears. Ollie's arrival in my life had been an irritation at first. Somehow, over the course of living and working with the man, his presence had morphed into a warm soft spot without me even realizing it. No longer an irritation, Ollie was just Ollie and I wasn't sure I wanted to go back to a time when I didn't know him.

But I sure as hell didn't know what to do about any of that.

"You see something happening between the two of you?" Julian asked.

Oh, something happened all right.

But I knew he meant more than physical.

I shrugged. "I do. But I don't know if it's the right decision. I don't have a great history with relationships. I don't know how long I'll stay at the center. I don't know if I can get into something and then room with the guy if things go south."

Julian nodded. "You can work elsewhere and still be

with Ollie. Neither of you have a great history with relationships, but maybe that's because you were waiting for each other. And avoiding something just because it *might* go bad isn't the best way to live your life."

I pondered Julian's words as the crew reappeared and we settled in for slices of pizza, fries, and a few shared fountain sodas.

"Two drinks of water for every drink of pop," Dean warned. "Dehydration isn't fun."

"Yes, Dr. Pierce," Lucas teased.

The rest of the day was truly picture perfect. If we'd spent months planning the day, we couldn't have lucked out and gotten better weather. The lines really weren't too bad, the sun was hot, but the breeze was nice, and we didn't have to worry about rides shutting down because of the rain.

Ollie was his usual flirty self and I realized his brief, barely-there touches were almost more distracting than if he'd just cupped my junk and kissed my neck. Seriously, he was driving me insane—and he knew it if the sorry-not-sorry faux innocent smirk and lash batting he gave me was anything to go on.

Pinky fingers brushing as we walked.

Arms bumping together.

Fingers digging into my shoulders as he steadied himself on the railing while we waited in line.

A step too close into my space so his back and ass pressed against mine when he was talking to Leighton while a line crawled through its maze.

The brush of his chest against me when he leaned

across to flick a non-existent piece of fuzz from Leighton's hair.

All.

Damn.

Day.

Before meeting Ollie, that type of blatant flirting would have annoyed the hell out of me and turned me off completely.

After Ollie—thanks to getting to know him, spending time with him in different settings, and especially taking a break and getting to recharge with him on our little birthday trip—I found myself wanting to grab his hand, yank him to a hidden corner, and have my way with him.

The thought made me chuckle. I knew Ollie would be one hundred percent on board with that idea.

"What's funny?" Ollie asked as we waited for Dean and Lucas to exit the gift shop at the end of a coaster we'd ridden three times.

I wanted to tell him.

Wanted to just throw caution to the wind and see what might happen.

Ollie wanted it.

LuLu was in support.

The guys seemed to think it was inevitable.

My body was in complete agreement—my heart was slightly less sure—but my head just couldn't stop the worry.

Instead, I just shrugged. "Just saw a kid doing something his parents definitely won't like."

Ollie smiled. "Do you want kids one day?" he asked, taking me completely off guard.

Without even thinking, without weighing what the answer might mean for whatever the little spark between us was trying to be, I shook my head. "No. Kids aren't for me. I know that's weird since I've basically spent my entire career with kids in one capacity or another—even in high school, I was a camp counselor for a couple summers —but having children of my own isn't anything I want."

Ollie's face showed understanding and relief. "I completely get that. I have a great job where I get to spend all day with kids—and I love it, I really do, the kids are amazing—but at the end of the day, I want to go home and just be me." He shrugged, watching some kids playing. "I think a lot of it has to do with my childhood. My mom sucked. My first several years had the capacity to screw me up beyond repair—and in some ways, I wonder if I'll ever escape the damage her choices did to me—but I lucked out with Dad and Julian taking me in. I just don't want the responsibility of having kids of my own. I love spending the day with them, watching them learn, seeing when they reach a pivotal moment, but I want to send them to their own homes and have Ollie time when the day is done." He huffed. "Damn, that sounds selfish, huh?"

I shook my head. "No, I don't think it's selfish. I think it's realistic and I get it. Not everyone is meant for parenting—even though I think you'd be good at it—just like not everyone is meant to go to college or get married or do any number of things our society has trained us to believe are *the norm*." Gesturing toward the kids, I went on, "I think our backgrounds are pretty similar in a few ways and I completely understand where you're coming from. Kids aren't for everyone and I don't feel like my life is lacking without them."

As midday turned to afternoon and then into evening, our group continued to ride as many coasters as possible. My voice grew hoarse, my feet were killing me, I had a general grimy feeling coating my skin, and I knew I wouldn't want to do the amusement park thing every day, but damn, the entire experience turned out to be the most fun I'd had in a long time.

Sticking to our plan, we stayed until the park closed, the gates shutting behind us as we headed toward the parking lot.

"Don't know about you," Julian murmured as we loaded into the van, "but I'm grateful we've got showers and beds ahead of us. Not sure I could make the drive tonight."

"Agreed," Lucas said. "Damn, I'm beat."

We made a stop at a fast-food place and ordered a late-night snack before pointing the van in the direction of our room for the night.

Leighton and Jett doubled up in the shower again, but they were obviously just as worn out as the rest of us because they only took long enough to wash away the remnants of the day before exiting and crawling into bed.

The rest of us made quick use of the two bathrooms and were soon all crashing into our big, comfy beds. With alarms set—but not *too* early—and plans in place to pack up, check out, and hit the road before stopping for breakfast, we switched off lights and let the blanket of happy, sated exhaustion settle over the apartment.

Just as I was about to sink into sleep, Ollie shifted and

moved entirely too close to me. "Happy birthday, birthday buddy," he whispered, his minty breath whispering over my cheek as he leaned in, the warmth of his body only centimeters away, the sweet strawberry of his shampoo tickling my nose.

Assuming he'd waited until midnight to share birthday wishes with me, I smiled into the dark. "Happy birthday," I replied, still unable to wrap my head around the fact we shared a birthday. That was crazy, right?

"Did you have fun?" Ollie asked, keeping his voice soft and low even though gentle snores and deep breathing could be heard from the rest of the guys.

"I did," I admitted.

We fell into sleepy silence until Ollie spoke again.

"Since we're going to end up cuddled together anyway, can we just do it now?" Ollie's voice held hope and vulnerability. "Maybe it's just for the weekend, but I really liked being in your arms."

Fuck.

The man was going to be the death of me.

I liked it too I wanted to say.

Instead, I pushed away the warning bells in my head—focusing for the moment only on how badly I wanted to feel him against me—and scooted closer,

Ollie scrambled to roll away from me, pressing his back to my front, and burrowing against me.

As if two puzzle pieces finally clicked together, every cell in my body gave a happy, contented sigh at the touch.

Ollie took my hand and tucked it against his chest.

I wanted to say something.

But what?

This is nice, but don't get used to it?

I'm not sure this is the smartest idea?

Tomorrow, we go back to...whatever it was we had before?

My head had all sorts of ideas on what to say.

My heart and body argued it wasn't necessary. Or, more accurately, my heart and body wanted to say something along the lines of *I like this. Maybe we can see where it goes once we're back home.*

In the end, I just let myself enjoy the warmth of Ollie wrapped in my arms as I drifted off to sleep. We could worry about the rest of it later.

Waking up with Ollie in my arms for a second day in a row had my head all kinds of fucked up. He felt so right pressed against me, but I just couldn't decide if us being together would be for the best—for either of us.

Luckily, with it being the day we headed home, I didn't have to worry about how badly I wanted to hold onto him for a while longer. The eight of us slowly rolled from bed and packed, stripped the sheets, locked the door, and loaded the van.

We drove for an hour before stopping for breakfast, picking fast food that time around in hopes of making our return trip quicker. We all had things to do on our Sunday before the work week started.

After breakfast, a grumbling Ollie tried to get comfortable in the van, but his sunscreen had failed the day before and he was sporting a pretty decent burn on his shoulders and neck.

After about thirty minutes of shifting and griping, he fell asleep and I found myself with a softly snoring Ollie pressed against my shoulder.

I couldn't even be upset about it—I even kinda liked it.

What the hell had the man done to me?

Once we got home, the eight of us trouped up to the apartment.

"Happy birthday," Lucas said, pulling first Ollie and then me into a hug. I'd never considered myself a hugger, but I found I didn't hate it. Several of my new friends were huggers.

Birthday wishes were given all around and Ollie and I thanked them for the weekend.

"Definitely need to do it again," Leighton said. "And a party up on the roof soon."

The eight of us went our separate ways for the rest of the afternoon.

Julian and Ollie were going to see their dad for a birthday meal.

Shaw cuddled up with a book in the living room.

Lucas and Dean went up to the roof to work out.

Pretty sure Leighton and Jett planned on fucking each other's brains out for the rest of the day.

I headed to LuLu's place.

Where my spitfire aunt proceeded to drill me about my weekend with Ollie and tsk at me when I said I wasn't sure about us getting together.

"Bash, no man has ever brought out this glow in you. Ollie is the first guy I've ever seen you bite back smiles over. He's made you happy, why can't you see that?" LuLu asked with a frown.

"He's just not what I had planned. How would it look? He's so much younger. We work together. What if I don't stay at the education center?"

LuLu waved me off. "One of the things I always tried to break you away from was worrying so much about what others think. Who gives a damn? You're not some celebrity in the paparazzi spotlight—and even if you were, I repeat, who gives a damn—you don't need to think that far ahead. He likes you. You like him. Let things happen and see where they go. If you find a different job, fine. He's not with you because of your job. If things go south, Julian has already said you could get out of your lease pretty easily." She patted my arm. "I just don't know what you're waiting for."

"Maybe I'm scared," I admitted softly, knowing LuLu was my safe space even though I hated looking vulnerable.

"Of what?" LuLu cocked her head.

"I think I'm worried it won't work out and this time I'll truly be heartbroken. After Randal, I was pissed off and it stung, but my heart wasn't broken." I ran a hand through my hair. "Or maybe I'm scared it will work out—I don't know that I have what it takes to be in a real and true loving relationship. And how much time have I lost out on love by avoiding anything close to *real*?"

"Bash, dear, your parents did you dirty and I'm sorry I couldn't save you from it all. But you are a kind, loving, genuine man and anyone would be lucky to call you their own." She winked. "I just so happen to think a certain red-haired beauty is the best choice for that job."

I couldn't argue with her.

We spent some time talking about roller coasters and a hike LuLu had been on recently. We ordered pizza and watched a movie. By the time I headed home, my heart was full after a weekend with the guys and LuLu. I don't think I'd ever realized just how much being connected to a group of people could brighten a person's outlook on life. Outside of LuLu, my blood family situation sucked, but thanks to her and my new-found *family*, a weight had lifted and my future looked brighter than ever.

And so much of that had to do with Ollie.

I took a shower and headed to bed, but I found myself tossing and turning until Ollie got home. I listened while he showered and then went to his room.

Arguing with myself over the best thing to do, I rolled from bed, and walked to his doorway. A dim lamp lit Ollie's room as he stood in the middle with a towel wrapped around his waist, shaking a bottle of aloe.

"Have fun with your dad?" I asked, smiling softly when Ollie jumped. He'd clearly been deep in thought.

He bit his lip, eyeing my bare chest and boxer briefs. "Yeah, it was fun. Dad's always a hoot."

"Roger is a good guy. I can see where you and Julian get your great personalities. You're both very different, but I see a lot of your dad in both of you." I edged into the room. "How's the burn?"

"It's not the worst I've ever had—at least I'm old enough and smart enough now to put sunscreen on, I was an idiot as a kid and thought a good burn would be the answer to my poor pale, freckled skin woes." He shook the aloe bottle. "This has taken a lot of heat out of it. It's mostly just uncomfortable now."

Questioning my every move, but unable to stop myself, I stepped farther into the room and took the bottle. "Want some help?"

Ollie glanced around with a smirk. "Are we filming a bad porn?"

I snorted. "Do you want help putting this on or not, Oliver?"

Ollie turned fiery eyes my way, his hands landing on the towel wrapped around his waist. "I'd rather have help taking something off."

"Behave yourself." I squeezed a large blob of aloe onto my palm and tossed the bottle aside. Rubbing the gel between my hands, I motioned for Ollie to turn around. Pressing the cold aloe to his red shoulders, I chuckled at his gasp. "Sorry. Hold still, let me get your neck."

"Did you come in here to apply first-aid to my shoulders or were you hoping for another show to participate in?" Ollie asked.

I didn't answer for a moment, just enjoying the glide of his skin under my hands. "Honestly, I don't know why I came in here. I should have just enjoyed the weekend, visited with LuLu, and gone to bed. Instead, I dragged my damn ass out of bed and butted my nose where it doesn't need to be."

"I can get the dildo out…" Ollie suggested.

Ignoring his words, I blurted out, "I'm sorry for the other night."

"How many times do I have to tell you, it wasn't a bad thing. I wanted it. It was hot."

Finishing with his shoulders and neck, I wiped the rest of the aloe on his towel. "I could have at least kissed you before shoving my dick down your throat."

Ollie turned to face me, his hand coming up to brush

hair from my face. "You could kiss me now," he answered, his soft words going straight to my balls.

"What are we doing, Oliver?" I asked, my voice gruff, the question laced with uncertainty and hope.

"I think we're wrapping up a great weekend with a long-overdue kiss and maybe some birthday head," Ollie murmured, stepping close and wrapping his arms around my neck as he nuzzled my jawline.

"And that's all?" I wasn't sure if I meant *that's all* in regards to blowjobs and nothing more or what was happening between us, and I wasn't sure it mattered.

Ollie seemed to grasp on to the what was happening between us part. "I guess that depends on what you want. Casual works for me if it's all you can give. Honestly, it's all I've had in me in the past." His breath whispered over my cheek, sending tingles through me. "But if I had my way, we'd be letting loose and seeing just how far things might go. We'll never know unless we try."

"I don't know how much I have to give," I said.

"At this point," Ollie's words were warm against my ear, "I'll take whatever I can get."

"That's not fair to you," I protested, fighting the urge to hold him close and never let go.

"How 'bout you let me decide what's right for me, I'm a big boy." His teeth teased over my ear lobe. "Call me optimistic—maybe I'm putting way too much faith in fate —but I can't help but hope we'll find out giving what we've got is enough to see us through."

No longer able to fight the pull, I snaked an arm around his waist and pulled him close, dropping my head to press our lips together. Ollie's little gasp was enough to allow my tongue entrance, and I groaned at the slick heat of his mouth. He tasted of mint and sweetness, and I wanted to spend the rest of the night feasting on him.

Two things occurred to me as our mouths mated.

One, I wanted him. Wanted him more than any man before. And I wanted him as more than sex, more than playing a part, more than painting a picture of fake perfection. I wanted Ollie as a friend, as a lover, as a partner—I wanted him by my side no matter what people thought, no matter what job I had. There was no way I could let go of him, my heart would shatter in a million pieces if my inability to commit sent him into the arms of someone else.

Two, oh, hell. I couldn't even remember what the second thought was. All I knew was kissing Ollie was my new favorite activity and I never wanted to stop.

"Let me suck you off," Ollie begged against my lips when we finally broke apart.

"Wanna taste you, too," I said.

Ollie shucked the towel, locked the door, and made his way to the bed. "Take 'em off."

It took a moment for my head to catch up, I was too busy ogling Ollie's gorgeous nakedness, his hard, thick cock, and the tight thatch of dark auburn curls at the end of that glorious treasure trail.

I yanked my boxer briefs off and joined him on his bed, pushing all other thoughts from my head, promising myself Ollie and I could figure out whatever happened from this point on.

Ollie pushed me to my back and rolled on top of me. "Really want to straddle you and ride that cock, but birthday bjs can be our new thing. Couples who give head together, stay together and all that."

I snorted. "That's not a thing."

"It's *our* thing now, live with it." He kissed me, delving his tongue between my lips, exploring my mouth as he rocked our cocks together.

We broke apart, breathing heavily, and Ollie shifted his head toward the foot of the bed, lining up his mouth with my cock and putting his hard shaft right in line with my mouth. Stretched out on our sides, we swirled our tongues and took each other deep. Hips bucking, cocks thrusting, mouths sucking as soft whimpers and desperate grunts filled the air.

For a brief moment, the image of Ollie doing this with other men flashed through my head. I hated it. If I had my way, Ollie would never touch another man. My heart and body screamed *he's mine* and a powerful possessiveness rushed through me. I slicked a finger with spit and teased between Ollie's ass cheeks, loving the catch in his breathing when I breached his hole with the tip of my finger.

We fell into a perfect rhythm, fists stroking, slits leaking, and throats swallowing around throbbing cock heads. I cupped Ollie's tight balls as I bobbed my head up and down his shaft, loving the whimpery groans he gave me. My own balls were just as tight and I knew neither of us would last much longer.

When Ollie gave a final thrust and unloaded into the back of my throat, my body shuddered and pumped my release onto his greedy tongue. Aftershocks racked our bodies as the orgasmic haze blanketed us.

We lay spent and sated for a moment before Ollie pulled himself from my mouth and shifted to my side, bringing our mouths together in a slow, lazy kiss. "Happy birthday," he murmured against my lips.

"Happy birthday," I replied with a soft smile.

"Do we wanna talk about what any of this means?"

I sighed. "Yes, but maybe not just yet." All of my thoughts and realizations were new and heavy and more than I'd ever dealt with over a guy. "Give it some time to simmer? I know I want more than just a wham-bam one-and-done, but I'm not sure I'm ready to get super deep with my words just yet. Can we think things over?"

Ollie nodded. "For sure. I think that's good. But know I'm on the same page, this feels like more than just quick and casual. Not that I've ever done more than just quick and casual, but maybe that's how I know it feels like more."

We were silent for several moments, just enjoying the contented closeness of our bodies.

"I feel like I need to tell you something so it doesn't come across like I hid it from you," Ollie said, popping up on his elbow to look directly at me.

"That's not ominous or anything," I deadpanned.

"It's nothing bad, just not something I want you to find out later when I can just tell you now."

"I'm listening."

"So, you know I've given and received *a lot* of head." There was that shot of possessive heat zinging through me. "Had quite a few fingers and dildos in my ass—although, admittedly, most of those were my own." Ollie cleared his throat, leaned down to tease my nipple with his tongue, and popped back up. Taking a deep breath, he said, "I've never had a real cock in my ass. So, I'm far from being a virgin, but my ass is like a distant galaxy—where no man has gone before. Unless we're counting fingers and tongues."

I hadn't been sure where he'd been going with the conversation, but my surprise was heavy. "Do you not like anal? I've been in relationships where the other guy just isn't a fan."

"No, I like it—at least with fingers and toys—I've just always freaked out before getting to that point. When you're not planning on anything lasting more than one or two hookups, it's easy to just stick to oral and say goodbye before getting to anything else. I don't actively avoid anal with other guys, I've just always been moving on before getting there."

"You've topped other guys?" For some reason, the thought of being the first to fuck his ass had me getting all sorts of hot and bothered.

"A couple times. I liked it—and I'm completely down with topping, especially if it's you—but I'm *all* for bending over for you."

"Noted," I said with a smile. "Maybe we just let that happen however it happens?"

"I like that plan. Sleep in here with me?" Ollie asked on a yawn.

"If we're late to work—"

"Shut it. We'll set an alarm, we're not going to be late," Ollie interrupted and pressed a kiss to my lips. "Early morning, shower together, grab coffee, get a good start on the week. We've got the meeting with Danica. We'll figure the rest out as we go along."

With my little wrecking ball wrapped in my arms, I pulled the blankets up and over us. I drifted to sleep wondering how in the world my life had changed so much —for the better—in such a short amount of time. So much for best laid plans and thinking I knew what my future held.

NINE

Ollie

HOLY.

Fucking.

Shit.

Being a persistent flirt paid off.

Okay, if I'm being realistic, being a good friend—getting to know Bash as a person—is likely what paid off the most, but my flirting didn't hurt.

That's my story and I'm sticking to it.

From the moment I met that man, I had a feeling something was different.

Meeting LuLu, finding out Bash and I had family who knew each other, discovering we shared the same damn birthday, it was all just too much. There was a definite reason we'd been thrust together.

Sure, maybe I added a bit of fun angst to the mix by offering to blow him before I knew he was my boss, but the rest of it was fate and I wasn't going to question it.

Our weekend together had been spectacular. I couldn't have planned it any more perfectly if I'd tried. He'd taken a while to get comfortable with the whole crew when everyone had been in the process of moving in—truly so many people moved in at pretty much the same time, it got a bit hard to remember who got there when—but the weekend trip had been proof Bash was desperate for his very own found family. I loved our little group could be that for him.

The night before, I'd come home from a birthday dinner with my dad and Julian, and had nothing really on my mind except bed and thinking about the week ahead. Then Bash had come into my room and my whole night had taken a turn for the better.

The next morning, waking up in Bash's arms—which was something I was getting very used to doing and wanted to make an everyday thing—it felt as if something big had shifted between us.

With any other guy before him, I would have prided myself on wearing him down and winning the chase—only to skip out once I'd got what I wanted—but with Bash, things were different. Yeah, persistence had been key, but patience had been a big part of it too. I think he'd needed to see things for himself and make his own decisions at his own pace.

Don't get me wrong, I didn't think we were walking down the aisle anytime soon—and I truly wasn't at a point where I wanted that, at least not yet—but Bash was different, more relaxed. And I was willing to be by his side while he settled into this new chapter of his life.

"Share a shower with me?" I murmured against his scruff as we stretched and came awake.

"Only in the interest of the environment," he answered

gruffly.

"Obviously."

We brushed our teeth, showered in mostly silence—mainly because our mouths were too busy kissing and sucking—and finished getting ready.

"Let's plan on going to get lunch today, or at least ordering delivery," I suggested. "I'm guessing the meeting might be stressful, gives us a reason to get out of the building if needed."

"That's not a bad plan, but I'm hoping it doesn't come to that." Bash pocketed his phone and we headed out the door. "Do you think Leighton is at the shop this morning?" he asked as we neared Cravin'-a-Cup.

"No, I think he's got the late shift. He's been working the afternoon and evening shifts more if he can."

Bash chuckled. "To match up more with Jett's hours?"

"Bingo."

"They're good together," Bash said.

"They are. At first, I was worried Leighton was going to get fucked over again—falling for straight guys is his weakness—but it worked out. Jett just needed the right guy to come along and help him realize his sexuality wasn't as straight as he thought it was. They're both still learning about themselves and each other, but I think they've got a strong foundation." I couldn't help but be over-the-moon for my best friend.

I ordered a butterfly pea flower tea with lemon and an iced chai latte. One for now, one for later. Bash ordered an Americano and two scones. After we paid and got our order, we headed toward the center.

"What about Shaw? I get this feeling his past is none too pretty," Bash said, sighing at the first sip of caffeine.

"Definitely. I mean, if we're being honest, you and I don't have the prettiest pasts, but I get the feeling his was even worse." The soft flavor of my tea teased at my tongue and I took a calming breath as we walked toward our day. "I don't feel like I'm in a position to just straight up ask him. I think if he were to tell anyone, it would be Julian. Hell, maybe he already has—Julian keeps shit like that on the down-low, doesn't even let his little brother in on the juicy stuff." I winced. "Not that I think Shaw's past is just good gossip fodder—that sounded bad after I said it. Sorry, I tend to let words fly and only think about how they sounded after the fact."

"I've noticed," Bash answered wryly and my face heated as I recalled my offers of sexual favors before we started working together. "I do think Shaw's had it rough. He seems to be settling in okay—sometimes I catch him looking around at everyone like he can't believe he got so lucky."

I clicked my tongue. "Can you blame him? Bitch, we're amazing." Twirling around with my tea cup in the air, I shook my ass as we reached the center and unlocked the door.

Following Bash to his office—not too worried about being seen stuck to him like glue because one, we had a meeting, and two, no one else was in the building yet—I put my iced chai in his fridge and flopped down to enjoy my butterfly pea flower tea.

Bash placed a scone in front of me.

"For me?" I asked in surprise.

"Did you think I got myself two?" he asked, his perfect ass perched on the edge of his desk as he studied me.

I shrugged, swiping up a dollop of glaze and licking it from my finger. "Thought you were hungry." I stood and moved between Bash's legs. "I know, I know, no workplace shenanigans," I whispered as he started to protest.

"This looks like shenanigans," he said.

"Just a quick one." I kissed him, hard and fast. "Thank you for the scone. That was nice."

As I started to move away, Bash tightened his hold on me, pulling me close and kissing me longer and deeper than before. Holy hell, the man could kiss. When we broke apart, he smiled and pressed his forehead to mine. "Turns out, I like doing nice things for you."

"First flowers, then chocolate milk, now a scone? Pretty soon you'll be showering me in diamonds and making me a kept man," I whispered with a grin, loving the huff of amusement escaping Bash.

"Keep dreaming," he said, closing his eyes as if savoring our closeness.

We enjoyed our little moment for the space of several heartbeats before pulling apart and returning to our breakfast.

"Danica is supposed to be here at ten. I'll text you when she gets here, but plan on being available," Bash said around a mouthful of scone.

"Will do. Kinda nervous, but also kinda pumped to get everyone on the same page and figure out what was going on back when I thought Elise was this great director."

Bash shrugged. "Maybe we'll find out there's another answer that doesn't paint Elise as the bad guy."

I narrowed my eyes. "You really think that?"

"No, not in the slightest, but I'm open to other options."

We finished our food as noises in the hallway indicated others were arriving.

With a quick kiss, I took my tea and left Bash alone in his office.

———

DANICA WAS A GORGEOUS, imposing, no-nonsense woman.

I liked her immediately.

And by liked her, I meant I was terrified of her.

"Mr. Mayer, it's nice to put a face with the name. Nice to meet you," Danica said, offering me her hand.

"It's Ollie, please. Nice to meet you," I said as I shook her hand.

We were in Bash's office and I remembered my iced chai from earlier.

I grabbed it from his fridge and took a seat.

Danica eyed my drink, but said nothing.

"Can I get you water? Coffee?" Bash offered.

"No, thank you." Danica smiled and tapped long fingernails on her notebook as she launched into how she came to take over for her father. "As you know, Dad has owned this place since its conception. The education center has been his baby from day one. It wasn't until the last couple years I started worrying about his capacity to keep things running well—make sound business decisions, that kind of thing—he's still going strong, especially at his age, but a few things have definitely started slipping. My mother finally convinced him to retire completely—they've taken off to Florida to live in a retirement community—and I took over." She cocked her head and glanced between us like she wanted to say something, but she pursed her lips and went on. "Sebastian, have you had a chance to delve into the financials since your arrival?"

Bash nodded. "I probably wouldn't have started with looking at the books, but Ollie mentioned something about budget cuts and that immediately got me suspicious."

"Why?" Danica asked.

Bash shrugged. "When your father hired me, he proudly told me of how well the place ran, how I'd have a generous budget to play with. So, the mention of budget cuts in a 'generous budget' had me questioning things."

"Did you find anything?"

"I did. I'm guessing it's the same thing you've come across now that you've taken over. Money is missing."

Danica sighed and nodded. "Yeah, that's the same thing I realized—I hoped you'd tell me something to disprove my theory. Any ideas?"

"I don't think there were a lot of people in on it. Maybe the accountant? But even then, that might have been just him willing to look the other way." Bash clicked a key to wake up his laptop—staff were supplied center-owned devices, they were decent, but could definitely do with some upgrades—and opened a drawer to pull out a folder. He flipped through papers in the folder until he found something with a header on it. "Lyle Dixon, Accountant," he read as he clicked keys on his laptop. "It would take more digging, but from a simple search, there is no Lyle Dixon, Accountant."

"That's the same conclusion I came to," Danica said. "I think Elise was skimming money from the center, fixing the books, using a fake accountant to make things look official. Dad has always been way too trusting—he didn't question when Elise started using *Lyle* after our family accountant retired." She turned to me. "Do you have any contact with Elise?"

I shook my head. "No. Like I told Ba—Sebastian—Elise had access to our contact info, but we didn't have hers. She was nice, friendly, left people alone to do our jobs. She was here one day and gone the next. Took a while, but Mr. Eller finally reached out and told us not to worry, he already had a suitable replacement lined up. We never heard what happened to her, she was just gone."

Danica grimaced. "Yeah, that was when I really started getting concerned. Wasn't until Dad hired Sebastian that I found out Elise had disappeared. Dad said he got an email from her saying she'd no longer be working for the center. Nothing else. I've tried to have someone look into it—see if they can figure out where she is—but the police are no help since there's no proof of anything illegal. I hadn't gone as far as hiring private help just yet. I wanted to meet you and see if you'd come to the same conclusions as me."

"The books will help bring the police on board, I'd think," Bash said.

"Definitely. Maybe with what you and I both found, the fact she just up and disappeared, and the initial search of Lyle Dixon showing up as a dead end as far as accountants go, we'll get some answers." Danica stood up and we followed suit. "I'm not thinking this will be a quick and easy thing, but I think we've got enough to get the ball rolling. She stole from my family, stole from our employees, from our students—I don't want her getting away with it. It's not like she took enough to live high for the rest of her life, but she needs to face consequences."

Danica walked toward the door, but paused and glanced back between us.

"I was planning on talking to you about a no fraternization policy being put into the employee handbook," she started and cocked a brow at Bash. "But I'm wondering if one, that's even a problem, and two, if it's too late."

"It's not a problem," I blurted. "Fraternizing, I mean. It happens—like, it definitely happens—lots of fraternizing. Fraternization beyond the wildest fraternization." The words tumbled from me, I'd lost all semblance of control.

Bash turned wide, stunned eyes my way, his face begging me to shut up.

Danica smirked.

"What I mean," I attempted to salvage the situation, "is the center is full of professionals and no one here would let anything like a bit of fraternization get in the way of doing our jobs."

"Please stop," Bash muttered.

"Stopping now," I said.

A huff of laughter escaped Danica.

"As long as I don't start hearing complaints—and as long as any others keep their fraternization as *professional* —I can hold off on instituting the policy."

"Let's say you start the policy, anyone who was fraternizing *before* the policy was put into place would be safe, right? I mean, you can't break up a couple who got together before there was a policy—before they even worked together. Right?" None of us missed the way my voice squeaked.

"I think that couple would likely be safe," Danica answered with a brief smile. "If either of you hear anything about Elise, think of anything, or just have questions, feel free to reach out. Sebastian, you don't have to question every employee who worked here under Elise, but if you pick up any details, pass them along. I'll keep you updated on what I find out from my end."

We saw her to the door.

Bash turned toward me.

"Oliver."

"Sebastian."

He huffed and rolled his eyes. "Next time, I'm taping your mouth shut. Fraternization beyond the wildest fraternization?"

"Sorry, I freaked out. Do you think she got the hint because my chai was in your fridge? Is that a dead giveaway?" I bit my lip. "*My chai was in your fridge.* It has a nice ring as a euphemism."

Bash snorted.

Ignoring the fact we were in the hallway, I took advantage of the darkened corner away from prying eyes. "Hey, hot stuff," I murmured with a grin, moving into his space and pressing my body against his. "You can put your chai in my fridge anytime you want."

Bash's hand brushed against mine. For a brief moment, I thought he was going to give in. But he gave my hand a squeeze and muttered, "Professional. We'll continue this at home." As he walked away, Bash turned around and smirked. "I don't even drink chai."

I gaped after him. "That's not what I meant and you know it."

———

"Can you believe we have the entire apartment to ourselves?" I asked Bash a few days later as I walked into my room in the late afternoon after my extra-long shower —come on, when one thinks they may be getting railed, one takes care to prepare certain body parts, and that preparation takes a bit of time.

Bash wore only boxer briefs and smelled of his lemon and sage soap.

It wasn't often anyone got the place completely to themselves.

Not that we were going to parade naked through the living room or prepare a feast for ten in the kitchen, but it was nice to know any bedroom activities could get as loud as needed.

Jett and Leighton didn't seem to worry much about the

volume of their bedroom behaviors, and we razzed them plenty for it.

If I had to make a guess—just from his personality and the two times I'd had his cock down my throat—I didn't think Bash was super loud in bed, but you never really knew until you got right down to it. He definitely wasn't one of those who roared or screamed.

I'd had years of practice keeping my noises to myself, but I couldn't promise I wouldn't be grunting and groaning up a storm once Bash deflowered my virgin ass.

Not gonna lie, I was slightly nervous.

But in a good way.

It was mostly excited anticipation causing butterflies to work themselves into a frenzy in my gut.

I'd taken a fairly large dildo on more than one occasion.

I knew Bash would be as gentle as I needed him to be.

I think I was mostly nervous *he* wouldn't like it.

I'd finally gotten him to admit there was at least a little something between us—spent so much time trying to woo him into my bed...or at least into my ass...now I was worried I wouldn't live up to my own hype.

"You okay?" Bash asked, wrapping his arms around me and pulling me with him onto the bed, my damp towel coming undone and slipping from my hips.

"Just worrying I worked so hard to get to this point I maybe oversold myself a bit," I said, cuddling close and tangling our legs together.

"Never. We've got time, we don't have to do anything if we're not into it."

I huffed and caressed a hand over my ass. "I'm not

wasting a perfectly good prep on taking our time. You will plow me and plow me good."

Bash laughed. Like a full-on, out loud laugh, and pulled me in for a kiss. "Never let it be said I wasted a good prep, let's get to plowing."

We kissed for several moments.

And then kissed for several more.

Somewhere between tongues mating, hands exploring, and hips thrusting, my worry flew out the window, replaced by a deep, fiery desire.

I wanted what I'd never had, but more importantly, I wanted it to be with Bash.

The first and only man I'd ever let worm his way into my heart and life enough for me to consider sticking around.

"Fuck," Bash murmured against my lips, nipping and sucking. "Condom? Lube?"

"Drawer."

He grabbed the supplies and tossed them on the bed before flipping me to my back, shucking off his underwear as he tossed my towel aside, and kneeling between my spread legs. "It's like a damn buffet," he said, skimming his hands up and down my thighs. "I'm starving, but I don't even know where to start."

"Go for the prime rib while it's hot and ready. You can always come back for pizza or a dinner roll later." I stroked my cock, my greedy ass clenching as I eyed Bash's length. He wasn't romance novel huge—for which I was grateful—but my mouth watered as I watched his hard, throbbing cock bob between his legs.

"Did you just compare your ass to prime rib?" Bash asked, eyebrow cocked and smirk firmly in place.

"Yes, yes, I did. Hand jobs are dinner rolls. Blow jobs are pizza. My ass is prime rib." I wrapped my legs around him and pulled him down, our chests pressed together. "You're the one who started the buffet metaphor, I just took it and ran. Come on, keep up."

We rutted together, our pre-cum blending as the friction built and our mouths became one.

"You wanna ride me? May give you more control, ease the pain," Bash suggested.

"Yeah, but not yet."

Bash gripped the back of my neck and deepened the kiss, thrusting our cocks together to the point I worried I'd blow my load before we got much further.

But he ended the kiss, allowing me to get myself somewhat under control, and pressed his lips to my heated skin as he made his way down my chest, my torso, my groin, nipping at my inner thighs. Before I had time to process his intent, Bash flipped me to my stomach and settled between my legs. Hot, open-mouthed kisses were pressed to my rounded ass cheeks before he parted me and swiped his tongue over my hole.

"Fuck," I grunted, rocking my cock into the mattress.

Bash worked me open, his tongue swirling and probing.

"Fuck," I repeated. "Please," I begged, gripping the sheets.

He moved, spreading his weight over my body, pressing his cock between my ass cheeks as he tilted my head for a deep, sloppy kiss. "What do you want?" he asked, his voice gruff and desperate.

"In me," I panted, licking into his mouth, chasing the flavor of sex on his tongue.

Bash rolled to his back and made short work of sheathing his dick.

I smeared lube on my well-eaten ass and coated his shaft, teasing extra slickness over his cockhead and loving the way Bash moaned.

Moving to straddle his waist, I reached behind to guide his cock to my hole. Working it in, lowering myself inch-by-glorious-inch, I realized silicone was nice, but Bash's dick was my new favorite toy. The burning stretch took my breath, but the fullness—the feeling of being complete—set fire through to my veins. I paused, allowing my body to adjust, and stared down at Bash.

This was different.

Different *good*.

Holy hell, emotions nearly knocked me over.

Bash was so much more than a quick mutual jerk-off or good head.

Maybe my mind was scrambled due to his thick cock gliding in and out of my ass as I rocked myself on him, but Bash was *real*. He meant something to me beyond quick, easy, unattached sex.

Tears stung my eyes at the realization of how well and truly fucked I was if things with Bash and I ever went south.

My heart had never gotten involved.

And now I knew why falling in love was the best and the worst.

"Fuck, Oliver," Bash gritted out, his fingers digging into my hips. "You good?"

I made a slight whimpering noise and continued to ride his cock, my own dick returning to life after a brief, deflating moment with the initial sting. "Wanna be under you, feel you all over me," I said.

Sudden loss filled me as I allowed Bash's cock to slide from my body, but I quickly moved to my stomach in the middle of the bed and spread my legs.

Bash moved between my spread thighs and parted my ass, teasing a finger over my desperate hole. He shifted so as to impale me once again, his body spread out over mine, arms wrapping under my pits and coming together at my chest, my back pressed tightly to his front. "This okay?"

"Fuck, yeah. Move. Wanna feel you come in me."

Bash set a smooth, steady rhythm, rocking and thrusting into me. My cock and balls begged for release, although I wasn't sure I could come in that position, but the sensation of Bash's shaft sliding in and out of me, brushing over my prostate, filling and stretching me, was so overwhelmingly good, I wanted nothing more than to lie there and take it.

Bash's movements increased in speed and power, his breathing coming faster and harder. "Fuck, Oliver. Fuck. Gonna come."

He held off for several moments before stilling, grunting softly as his cock throbbed deep in my ass, Bash's body tense as he shot his load.

With my cock aching for my own release, I groaned when he pulled from my body and rolled to his back, removing the condom and dropping it to the floor. Bash reached to stroke my cock before digging in the drawer and producing another condom. "In me. Now."

"You sure? Not too worn out?" I asked, rolling the condom down my length and applying lube.

"Wanna feel you," Bash answered, smearing lube against his tight pucker, spreading his legs in invitation.

I took my place between his legs, lined up my eager cock with his hole, and froze. "Do you need stretched?"

"I'm all relaxed from coming, just go slow," Bash said.

He pushed against me as I worked my cock into his impossibly tight ring of muscle. "This won't last long," I warned.

"Just wanna feel you in me," Bash said, reaching up to pull me down for a long, slow kiss as my tight balls pressed against his body. "Fuck," he muttered against my lips. "So good."

The couple times I'd topped before had been frenzied and fast and meaningless—I couldn't even remember the guys' names.

But this moment, the sweet ache in my ass, the sensation of completeness as our bodies once again became one, it was everything I hadn't known I'd been missing in my life.

Not just because it was good sex, but because it was Bash.

I went slow, knowing his body was spent and likely overly sensitive, thrusting gently into his tight heat. There would be time for hard and fast, but the orgasm that had been teasing right at the edge as Bash fucked me came rushing back with each and every glide of my cock into Bash's body.

His hands roamed up and down my back as we kissed, my hips slowing their thrusts and grinding into him as I chased my release. Bash gripped the back of my head and kissed me, sending fire to my balls as his tongue stroked over mine. "Come in me, Oliver," he demanded, pulling me close, pressing his forehead against mine as our hot breaths heaved and mingled.

With a final rotation of my hips, I stilled, my cock erupting as my balls emptied in spurt after spurt deep in Bash's body.

I stayed buried in him until my spent cock slipped out. Tossing the condom to the floor, I let Bash wrap me in his arms.

"That was good, right?" I asked.

Bash chuckled. "Better than."

"I think I definitely like the whole flip-fuck situation. It's like the best of both worlds."

Naked, warm, and exhausted, we curled into each other and drifted off to sleep despite a hint of light still coming through the window.

It was dark when I woke some time later, but the dick pressed against my ass caught my attention more than the time of night.

"Are you too sore?" Bash murmured against my ear, my back pressed to his front, his hard shaft nestled into my ass.

"Not up for a massive pounding, but I could definitely go again," I answered, stretching like a cat and rocking my ass against him. I felt around in the drawer and came up with a condom. "Need to stock up."

"Or we discuss it and get tested, maybe don't need them."

My eyes flew to Bash's.

"Just a thought," he said.

"I like it."

Fuck.

The thought of taking Bash bare had my cock surging back to life and my ass begging to be filled.

With the condom on, Bash lifted my leg, bending it and pressing it to the mattress. He pushed the head of his cock against my well-used ring of muscle, my body rejoicing as he entered me, filling me up, making me complete.

While riding Bash had been fun, there was something about the feeling of him pressed against me, the warm weight of his body on mine. With my chest partially against the mattress, my leg bent to support the position, and Bash's heat weighing comfortably down on me, I gave myself over to the sensation of his cock gliding in and out of my hole.

He was slow and gentle this time around. With soft kisses to my neck, Bash reached for my cock and stroked. "God, this ass. Love being inside you, so tight." He continued the long, slow thrusts. "Fuck."

When he cupped my balls and squeezed, I felt the familiar tingle at the base of my spine telling me orgasm was near. "Get me off," I whispered into the darkened room.

Bash complied, gripping my cock and stroking in the

same rhythm as his dick in my ass. "Come with me, Oliver," he demanded, his thrusts faltering, losing his rhythm. His cock throbbed in my ass as my own release flowed over his fist.

Several moments later, spent and sated in ways I'd never imagined—amazing what sex with emotions involved can do for a person—we dragged ourselves from bed and made our way to the bathroom to clean up.

The apartment was quiet, but a quick check of my phone proved it wasn't all that late. We'd started bedroom activities early and it seemed everyone was still out or at work.

"I'm starving," I told Bash as he finished up in the shower and I dried off. "Gonna walk to the coffee shop. Leighton's on and he'll give me leftovers he can't save at closing. You want a drink?"

"No caffeine, I'd be up until dawn and work would be a total bitch."

We'd been digging around, looking for things on Elise the last couple days after meeting with Danica. Hadn't really found anything earth-shattering.

A couple people had been suspicious of Elise.

Most had liked her.

There definitely was no accountant named Lyle Dixon.

Money had for sure been taken.

Elise was proving hard to find.

That was about all we had.

"I'll get whatever sandwiches and pastries he's got, and something decaf." I checked the time. "Gotta book it, they'll be starting their closing routine soon."

Bash leaned out of the shower, dripping water

everywhere, and I kissed him soundly. I was already liking this whole couple-y thing.

When I arrived at Cravin'-a-Cup, I immediately knew Leighton wasn't doing well. He got migraines—while he didn't get them *often*, maybe once a month or so, he got them enough for me to recognize one when I saw it—and from the look on his face, he had a doozy.

"Why didn't you ask to go home?" I said, the moment Leighton's pinched and pained expression landed on me.

"No one to cover. Just gonna finish up and then go home. Already called off for tomorrow—I'll be useless after this."

Sitting Leighton at a table, I politely explained the situation to a couple women sipping coffee and gratefully turned the sign to closed after they left, locking the door behind them.

"Not supposed to close early," Leighton protested.

"It's like ten minutes early. Your boss shouldn't have had you closing alone. Tell me what to do."

With Leighton's directions, I did a fairly decent job of closing down the shop. Anything I missed would be on the opening shift and they could kiss my ass; I needed to get Leighton home and in bed.

I helped him take off his apron, clocked him out, grabbed his phone and my bag of leftovers, and headed out the back door.

"Did you tell Jett?" I asked, holding Leighton's elbow and hating I could tell just how badly he hurt.

"No, he's got an appointment, no need to interrupt when I'm just going home to bed." Leighton's voice was laced in pain.

I shot off a quick text to Jett.

Me: Your boy's got a migraine. Taking him home.

Jett: Shit. Thanks. I'm done here, be home soon.

As we walked the shortcut from the shop to our place, I noticed a weird light in the education center's window. In Bash's office. Had he forgotten to turn off his lamp? The light wasn't bright enough to be anything more than something small.

I slowed our walk slightly and studied the light.

What the hell?

Probably nothing, but there was no reason for it to be on, and I didn't want something electrical overheating and causing a fire. Or even just wasting electricity. We wanted our money going to the students, not overactive utility bills.

I tapped out a quick text to Jett knowing he was likely nearby. Most everything on Cravenwood Block was nearby.

Me: Can you meet me and get him home? Something weird at the center I need to check out.

Jett: Yeah, I'm almost home. Where are you?

. . .

Me: Behind center, took shortcut.

"IF IT'S SOMETHING WEIRD, don't you think you should call the police?" Jett asked, scaring the shit out of me walking up behind us.

"Fuck, don't do that," I said, trying to calm my racing heart.

"Don't stand in the middle of a dark courtyard texting about weird stuff. Did you call the police?"

"Nah, I think Bash left a light on. Or the cleaning crew. I'll just go in, turn it off, make sure everything's turned off."

Jett looked at me skeptically, but his biggest concern was for Leighton who had curled against him and looked like death. "Okay, but I'm telling Bash."

I nodded. "Yeah, tell him I'll be right there. Give him this, we'll eat when I get home." I handed the bag of food to Jett.

I leaned in and kissed Leighton softly on the temple. "Love you, boo. Feel better. Holler if you need anything when you're back among the living."

Leighton attempted a smile and patted my face. "Love you."

I watched them walk away before walking to the back door of the center and entering my code. Nothing seemed amiss in the back entry or hallway, and I didn't plan to walk the whole building if I got to Bash's office and saw it was just a lamp left on accidentally. If something creeped me out, I'd call the police and Bash.

But honestly, the alarm system would have gone off if someone had broken in.

Right?

And the building was armed when I keyed myself in.

So, Bash likely just left the light on.

Or one of the cleaning crew turned it on to vacuum and forgot to turn it off.

All of the placating I was doing flew out the window the moment I walked into Bash's office.

There was a man.

Well, I assumed it was a man based on his size—huge, he was huge and dressed all in black.

His back was to me as he messed with something on the wall.

What the hell was he doing?

Who the hell was he?

And why the hell was I still standing there?

"Yeah, I'm ready. Give me the code. If they were stupid enough not to change the alarm system, I doubt they changed the safe." The man spoke into a phone tucked between his shoulder and ear. "Hell, maybe they don't even know it's here. Took me forever to find it."

That's when I noticed the large aerial photo of Cravenwood Block had been removed from the wall and propped up to the side. In the dim light, I could see a square hole in the wall where a safe sat.

Shit.

What was in the safe?

Who was this guy talking to?

It had to be Elise, right?

She'd be the only one to know about a hidden safe, the combination, and the code for the alarm system.

I wasn't stupid enough to think I could take this guy on my own—hell, I didn't even know if he had a weapon, all I knew was he was big enough to snap me like a twig— but I felt like I needed to keep an eye on him until the police could arrive.

Fuck.

Police.

Yeah, I needed to call them.

I reached for my phone, tapped out a quick message to Bash telling him someone was in his office—hoping Jett had filled him in enough he'd follow the somewhat cryptic words—and then switched to my phone keypad to dial 911. I'd have to walk out of the room to make the call, so I waited for just a moment to see if the man got into the safe.

Like in a movie, everything happened in slow motion in the next moment.

My phone—*not* on fucking silent—beeped with a random text.

The man startled and turned around.

He grunted when he saw me.

I held up my hands, backed up a few steps, before turning to run.

My back was to him, but I had to guess he charged me because I ended up slammed to the ground, the fall rocking my world as my forehead ricocheted off the corner edge of the door before hitting the floor with a thud like someone had dropped a watermelon.

Pain lanced through my head, like a sharp knife in the front and a wooden mallet in the back.

"Who the fuck are you?" the man growled.

"Fuck off, who are you?" I replied, feeling woozy and pissed from the head injuries.

"What? Oh, some kid snuck up on me," the guy said into the phone. "What? How the hell should I know? You're the one who used to work here, I'm just doing your dirty work." He turned his attention back to me. "What's your name?"

"Is that Elise? What's in the safe? Where is she?" I asked, ignoring his request about my name, trying to get my questions out despite my words feeling thick and not quite right.

"None of your business to the first two, and you won't need to worry about it for at least eighteen months," he said with a chuckle.

"Wait, what?" I asked, my pounding head trying to make sense of his riddle. I seriously felt as if I was going to puke. Something wet trickled down my temple and the back of my head hurt bad enough it *better* have been bleeding to match how badly it hurt.

The man grunted into the phone. "Huh? You ain't said nothing about hurtin' nobody." He watched me in the dim light while he listened to whoever was on the other end of the phone. "Yeah, yeah. Fine."

Without warning, a fist slammed into the side of my head.

My body fought to give in, but I attempted to sit up, I *had* to stop this man. What exactly I thought I would be able to do, I didn't know, but maybe Bash had called the police and they'd get here in time to catch the bad guy before he got to whatever was in the safe.

The man drew back his arm, but I wasn't quick enough.

He connected.

Hard.

That second blow was enough to send me into lala land.

I was out cold.

TEN

Bash

"HERE, Ollie said to give this to you and you could eat when he got home," Jett said, his arm around a visibly unwell Leighton.

"What? Where's he at?" A sensation of worry washed over me.

Why?

Ollie was a big boy, he could do whatever he needed to do.

But something niggled at me, telling me something wasn't right.

"He found Leighton with a migraine, was bringing him home, saw something weird at the center, handed Leighton off to me, and was going to go check out the center," Jett explained.

"Weird how?" I walked to the door to pull on a pair of shoes as I spoke.

"Said he saw a light. I told him to call the police, but he said it probably wasn't a big deal." Jett led Leighton toward their room, talking over his shoulder. "Said if he got there and something seemed wrong, he'd call the police."

"Thanks," I said, glancing down at myself and realizing I had on only boxers. I rushed to my room, yanked on a pair of pants and shirt, and headed toward the door.

I paused long enough to punch in 911 before heading down the stairs.

As I made the report of suspicious activity at the education center, a text from Ollie popped up on my screen.

Oliver: *Someone is in your office.*

FUCK.

I relayed the information to the 911 operator and urged them to get the police there as quickly as possible, agreeing to stay on the line until the police arrived.

As I ran toward the center, sirens filling the air as they approached, I begged the universe to please let Ollie be okay.

Because I needed him in one piece so I could break his damn fool neck.

I arrived at the front door just as officers were preparing to go in. I hung up with 911 and debated whether or not to call Ollie. If he was trying to hide, I didn't want his phone to ring.

"I'm the one who called it in," I announced to the officer in charge. "An employee texted to tell me there was someone in my office."

"Tell us how to get to your office," the man demanded. "And key in the code so we don't make noise breaking in."

With shaking hands, knowing they wouldn't let me go with them—and understanding why even though I hated it—I keyed in the code and stepped back.

"Straight in, take a left, then a right. I'm at the far end of the hall," I said to the officer.

He gave a quick nod and waved for two of his crew to follow him.

"Sir, I need you to step across the street, please. You may sit in the police car at that corner, but I can't have a civilian here. We don't know who is inside," a kind yet firm female officer said, leading me away from the center.

I took a seat in the police cruiser, huffing out a frustrated breath when she closed the door. I was helpless and scared.

Who was in the center?

Why?

Did Oliver see them and leave? Did he call the police too?

Was the person still there?

Wouldn't Oliver have called me if the guy ran out?

Fuck.

Something was wrong.

I could feel it.

I jumped when the radio crackled to life with a request for paramedics to enter the building.

Glancing toward the flashing lights, I realized an ambulance had arrived.

I fisted my hands and sent up every prayer I could

think of that Ollie would be okay. If he'd been shot, wouldn't the whole neighborhood have heard the noise?

I watched as two paramedics pushed a stretcher into the center.

A few moments later, police walked out with a very large man cuffed between them and led him to the back of a cruiser.

I jumped out of the car, trying to get a better look at the guy.

"Sir, I need you to get back in the car," the officer from earlier told me.

"No. Please, I can't just sit there. I'll stay over here, but I can't sit in the car." I turned pleading eyes her way. "Please. I'm the director of the center. The employee in there is my boyfriend. They're going to need to talk to me. I need information so I can fill in the owner."

She sighed and gestured that I could stay where I was.

Several moments later, when they wheeled Ollie from the center, nothing could have kept me from running to the back of the ambulance.

The police officer tried to stop me, but by the time she reached me, I had Oliver's hand in mine and he was smiling up at me—okay, it was more a grimace, but he was awake. She backed off and left me with the ambulance crew.

"What the hell happened? Who was that?" I demanded.

"Sir, we're taking him to the hospital. He's got two head wounds that need looking at—maybe an overnight observation," a paramedic said as the two women loaded the stretcher into the back of the ambulance.

"Can I go with him?" I asked, immediately missing the touch of Ollie's hand in mine.

"Please, let him go," Ollie said from inside the vehicle.

The paramedic waved me inside and I took a seat watching as the woman worked to establish vitals.

"I'm going to kill you," I muttered at Ollie's ear as I leaned close. "As soon as you're better from this, you're dead."

He chuckled, but groaned. "Don't make me laugh," he mumbled. "My head feels like it's going to explode."

"You're probably going to need stitches on your forehead, maybe glue," the paramedic said.

"Will you still love me with a scar?" Ollie asked, his eyes closed against the pain.

"Yes, you idiot, of course, I'll still love you," I answered automatically, squeezing Ollie's hand in mine.

"Love you, too," he murmured.

As we arrived at the hospital, I realized what we'd just said.

Fuck.

Did I love Oliver?

Hell, I did.

Probably wouldn't have admitted it for a long time, but it's funny what a scare will do for a person's level of commitment.

Not the most romantic way to go about declaring my love.

Shit, what if Ollie's injuries caused him not to remember telling me he loved me?

"You'll need to sit in the waiting room until we get him into a room," one of the women told me as they unloaded the stretcher. "We'll come tell you what we know before we leave."

I followed them in and quickly found myself left in the ER waiting room as Ollie was wheeled behind a curtain.

Taking the moment to regroup—somewhat calmer knowing Ollie was injured, but awake and talking—I pulled out my phone.

I called Julian first.

"Hello," he answered.

"Hey, you at home?" I didn't want to drop bad news on him if he wasn't in a good location.

"Yeah, just walked in. Why?"

"I'm at the hospital. Ollie was hurt. He's okay, I mean, he's hurt, but he was awake and talking when they brought him in. We're in the ER. They're getting him set up and then I can go back."

"Shit, what happened?" Julian asked and I heard the door open. I figured he was on his way back out of the apartment.

"I don't know the whole story yet. He was bringing Leighton home, saw a light on in the center, went in to turn it off, some guy was in my office." My phone beeped with a call from Jett. "Are you on your way?"

"Yeah."

"I'll look for you, got another call." I switched over to Jett's call. "Yeah?"

"What's going on? I heard the sirens and figured it was you. What happened?"

I repeated the little bit I knew. "I'll let you know once I'm back there to see him. If they don't want to keep him overnight, we'll be home later." I checked my watch. "Or, more likely, in the morning depending on how long this takes."

"Did you call Julian?"

"Yeah, he's on his way."

"I heard him come in and leave again. He'll tell Shaw. I'll make sure Lucas and Dean know." Jett paused and cleared his throat. When he spoke again, he was whispering and I pictured him checking in on Leighton. "Can we agree there's no reason to tell Leighton right now?"

"Definitely, let him sleep. He can't do anything here at the hospital. Fill him in once he's awake and coherent. He and Ollie can cuddle tomorrow as they rest."

Jett made a noise that sounded like agreement. "Okay, Shaw just walked in. I'll let him know."

I ended the call and looked up as the paramedics from earlier came into the waiting room. One of the women gestured to me and I joined them.

"You can go back. They've started fluids and they'll take him for a CT scan soon. Once they get that, they'll fix the gash on his forehead and probably get him some pain meds. I don't think the bump on the back of his head is open. If he has a concussion, they'll give you all the treatment procedures. Mainly, he'll need to rest."

As I said goodbye to the paramedics, I saw two of the police officers from the scene walking through the door. I waved and they walked to where I stood.

"Sorry, didn't catch your name earlier," the first officer said. "I'm Officer James and this is my partner, Rawlins. Can we ask some questions about what happened?"

"Better luck getting information from Oliver," I said,

gesturing toward the curtain. "They said I can go in. If he's up to it, you can ask him questions too."

Ollie's eyes were closed when we walked through the curtain. I didn't blame him, the lights were ungodly bright. "Hey," I said softly, taking his hand. "You feel up to questions before they take you for the CT scan?"

He glanced toward the officers and back at me.

For a brief moment, I panicked thinking maybe he didn't remember what had happened. Relief washed over me when Ollie nodded. "Yeah, sure." He squeezed my hand. "But I've got a question first."

"Anything."

"Did you really tell me you love me?" he asked with a crooked grin, a smear of blood on his banged-up forehead.

I laughed. "Yeah, I did. I also told you I was going to kill you for going in there alone—or at all. You should have called the police first." All that fear came rushing back. "Damn it, Oliver. That was so fucking stupid."

He sighed. "I know. Bad decision on my part. But I'd prefer to focus on the fact you love me and we should let these nice officers ask their questions instead of dwelling on any murders. You love me, you're not going to kill me."

The officers launched into information-gathering mode. I filled them in on the missing money and our suspicions about Elise. Ollie told of finding the man, what he said to the other person on the phone, and the safe.

"The suspect had the safe open when we arrived," Officer James said. "He was loading money into a bag. The center is going to have to be closed tomorrow. Can you contact the owner, we'll need her there. We need to look into the thief, the person on the other end of the phone, and the money."

Ollie huffed. "I hate you have to close the center, even if it's just for a day. The kids will be so upset."

Officer Rawlins smiled understandingly. "My own kids go there, so I know there will be a bunch of sad kids. We'll do our best to have everything wrapped up as soon as possible. May have to barricade your office, Mr. Thomas, but the center can likely open day after tomorrow."

The officers asked a few more questions and gave us their cards before heading out with promises to see us tomorrow—well, *me* because Ollie wasn't going anywhere but his bed.

An orderly came to wheel Ollie to his CT scan.

I sat in the crappy little chair and called Danica. About halfway through the conversation, Julian popped his head through the curtain and I waved him in.

"Yeah, we'll see you tomorrow. I hate this happened, but maybe it's a step in the right direction to figure out where Elise is and get her punished for what she did." I ended the call and stood up to shake Julian's hand, but the man pulled me into a hug.

"Is he okay?" he asked quietly.

"Yeah, already cracking jokes. The nurse said the CT scan is a standard procedure for head injuries. I think he'll get stitches on his head. I'm hoping they let him come home. Maybe we can sell them on it because he has seven roommates and one of them is a doctor." I stretched and yawned. "I need to call Angela. She works the front office and has all the contact information for the families. The center has to close tomorrow and we need to get the information to parents as soon as possible."

By the time I'd filled Angela in and been assured she'd take care of it, Julian had found us some somewhat-decent coffee, called his dad, and Ollie was being wheeled back into his little cubicle.

While Julian hugged his little brother, scolded him for walking into a dangerous situation, and told him he'd need to answer to Roger, a text showed up on my phone indicating Angela had sent out a mass text to the parents. I knew she was also going to email and call. I felt confident she'd take care of the issue quickly and efficiently.

"Okay, let's get you closed up here," a nurse said brightly as she bustled into the room.

"Will I be able to go home soon?" Ollie asked.

"We'll see what the doctor says after she looks at the scans."

The nurse decided Ollie's cut could be glued together rather than stitched and chatted about not touching it or getting it wet for the first twenty-four hours. "No soaking it in water, but with it on your head that should be pretty easy. You'll hopefully have less of a scar with the glue than with stitches."

Thirty minutes later, the doctor came in.

"Mr. Mayer, you have a very mild concussion. If it weren't for the fact you have *two* head injuries, I'd almost lean toward saying you don't have a concussion, but we're going with *very mild* as a precaution. Overall, I'd say you were lucky. Neither bump to the head did too much damage and you should be back on your feet within about three days—of course, taking it easy for the next few weeks, but you won't have any work restrictions unless you do extremely strenuous activities at work."

"No, I'm the director of the music program at the Cravenwood Education Center," Ollie explained.

"My niece goes there, loves it." The doctor made a few notes on her tablet. "The nurse will bring you your papers and you'll be on your way in a bit."

When the nurse arrived, she went over the care instructions.

"So, he can sleep?" Julian asked.

"Yes, not sleeping isn't really part of the protocol much these days. His concussion is very mild. Resting is best for him—I want you *in bed* for the next two days," she said, making stern eye contact with Ollie. "You can get up on the third day, but don't get too crazy. After that, let your body dictate what you're able to do."

"We live with a doctor," I said.

That seemed to please the nurse and she had Ollie sign his papers and handed him a bottle with enough pain meds to get him to tomorrow along with a paper prescription to fill at the pharmacy.

"I brought the truck," Julian said when the nurse asked how we were getting home.

"Damn, good thinking. Thanks." The ER wasn't terribly far from Cravenwood Block, but no way Ollie could have walked that distance. He probably would have tried, but there was no way I was letting him.

The nurse ushered Ollie into a wheelchair and pushed him toward the doors. She waited with us while Julian went to get the truck and waved us on our way once Ollie was safely tucked in the middle of the cab.

By the time we got home, both Ollie and I were about to drop.

I helped him brush his teeth and wash his face, avoiding his cut.

He held plastic wrap and a towel over his forehead while I washed the blood from his hair and soaped his body. He waited patiently for the few moments it took me to wash and rinse my own hair and body, and then we climbed out of the shower.

I got Ollie dried and dressed and settled him in bed before grabbing water so he could take his medicine. I figured it would knock him out pretty good and I was grateful he'd get the rest he needed. I set an alarm and cuddled in next to him.

"I'll have to get up and head to the center tomorrow," I whispered. "If Leighton's feeling better, I'll have him come in and you two can sleep off the worst of what ails you."

"Sounds perfect," Ollie sighed. "I'm sorry for scaring you."

"I'm sorry it took being fucking terrified to realize how much you mean to me." I pressed a kiss to his temple.

"I'm just glad we love each other," Ollie murmured. "You know, I kinda think we click so well because of our pasts."

I waited to see if he was just rambling or if he had more to say.

"I mean," he continued. "We both know what it's like to

be in that terrible position where you're supposed to love your parents. You want to love them. But you know they hurt you, you know they hurt others. You know deep down they aren't good people. And you're plagued by guilt and confusion trying to figure it all out. If you love them like you're taught you're supposed to, you're loving someone who is so damn shitty. If you don't love them, because they're bad news, you're left feeling like a total piece of crap for not loving your parents. It's a vicious cycle."

I took Ollie's hand. "What brought on these thoughts?"

He sighed again. "Knowing you'd be by my side. Seeing my brother at the hospital. Knowing the guys would be there for me. Knowing Dad will be beating down the door to bring me chicken soup and shit. It all made me think of how my mom likely wouldn't have even shown up if I got hurt. That thought led to me thinking about your past and wondering why we seem to get each other so well. I'd never let myself love anyone outside of Julian and Dad—and I blame my mom for that. I think you've been in a similar situation, not truly opening your heart to anyone but LuLu. It makes sense our hearts would kinda take refuge in each other."

By that point, his words were slurring a bit and I wondered if he even knew what he was saying—but his words made sense. Even though almost twenty years separated us, we had a lot of the same shit in our pasts.

"Shhhh, get some rest. If you follow doctor's orders, I'll tell you all about how much I love you."

"Sounds amazing, I love that for me," he mumbled

before cuddling into his pillow and falling into a deep sleep.

It took a while for my brain to stop buzzing, and I knew work was going to be a bitch, but I finally fell asleep with Ollie safe in my arms.

The next morning, I helped Ollie use the bathroom, brush his teeth, and get his medication down.

Jett was going to drop off the prescription as he went to get breakfast.

Leighton took a shower and shuffled into Ollie's room with a blanket and pillow.

When I left, the two friends were snuggled together under their blankets for a cat nap before Jett returned with their breakfasts.

I knew from hearing Leighton talk that the day after the migraine was almost as bad as the migraine itself. He called it a migraine hangover, so I knew he and Ollie would definitely be taking it easy for the day.

They looked cute as hell and I snapped a picture which I sent to Ollie with a text saying, *"You two look cute and you better rest all damn day."*

Then I headed off to work.

Danica and I spent the entire day with the police and by the time they headed out, we actually had quite a few answers thanks to a lot of digging by the police department.

Elise Montgomery wasn't who we thought she was.

With some deep diving in systems Danica and I didn't have access to, the officers were able to connect Elise Montgomery to several aliases which were wanted in multiple crimes—all dealing with tax fraud, money misappropriation, embezzlement, and credit card fraud. Her real name was Linda Baylor and the day she disappeared from the education center was the day she was taken in for embezzlement under one of her other aliases.

The woman had at least six different names and a list of crimes a mile long in addition to warrants for her arrest in at least seven states. She'd been convicted of at least three instances of tax fraud under three different names, embezzlement under two names, and money misappropriation under all six of her names, but she'd been lucky as hell both running from and evading police in addition to escaping police custody and hiding in plain sight.

The day she didn't show up at the education center was the day everything caught up to her.

Elise—Linda Baylor—was now serving eighteen months for one conviction with at least eleven other cases being brought to court. From what our officers were able to find, now that she'd been caught, she wasn't likely to escape years and years of punishment for her crimes.

The man she'd contacted on the outside—the one who'd been in my office—was Ralph Floyd. He threw Elise under the bus the moment he was taken into custody. As a petty thief, he'd do some time, but his statement against Elise saved him from a potentially longer stint.

Ralph reported Elise had someone watching the computers at the center. The moment I'd searched for her name and Lyle Dixon, Elise was informed. She then used her contacts to hire Ralph to break into the safe. Elise had left a lot of the money she'd stolen from the center in the safe and was planning to move it a bit at a time to a different location.

Unfortunately for her, she was sent to prison before she got a lot of it moved.

Mr. Eller didn't know about the safe so Danica and I deduced Elise might have had it installed unbeknownst to anyone.

There was a lot of work and cleaning up to be done with the books—Danica was turning all of that over to a legit and highly experienced accountant with whom she'd work with for however long it took to straighten everything out.

The missing money would take a while to get back— what was found in the safe would come back to the center once it was no longer evidence, but there was no telling how long that would take.

The money Elise had managed to transfer out would take longer and be tied up in court proceedings for quite a while.

But the education center was doing well despite Elise's thievery and we'd be able to open up the next day.

Danica planned to speak individually to each employee the next day—she wanted them to feel safe and secure in their workplace, wanted to give them a chance to voice concerns.

"Let's call it a day. We'll be back in business tomorrow. I'll get someone to come reset the code on that safe if you want," Danica said as she packed up her laptop.

"No, I'd rather it be removed if that's possible," I said. "I don't want anyone thinking I've got anything to hide."

Danica nodded. "I'll have it removed." She paused at the door. "How's Ollie?"

"He's good. Been resting all day based on doctor's orders. He'll be out the rest of this week, but can return next week as long as he's feeling up to it." We'd been texting off and on during the day, and Dean had let me know Ollie was doing well. Julian had checked in on his brother several times.

I had a feeling the next day would be the more difficult one for keeping him in bed. Leighton would likely be back at work and Ollie would be getting restless.

"Can I ask you something?" Danica asked.

"Sure."

"You don't have to tell me, but I got the feeling when I read through your resume and talked to you on the phone you maybe weren't planning to be here very long." She cocked her head, studying me. "But maybe I was wrong?"

I smiled and sighed. "No, you were right. But things have changed. I went from thinking this job, this place, these people were all just a stepping stone for my career, but I see things differently now. I have every intention of spending as long here as you'll have me."

Danica smiled. "That's good to hear, we're lucky to have you. I look forward to building this place into something even bigger and better with your leadership." She reached out and shook my hand. "Can I be nosy and ask if this decision has anything to do with a certain red-haired cutie you may or may not be fraternizing with?" A grin teased her lips.

I snorted. "Fraternization beyond the wildest fraternization."

We both laughed.

"Yeah, he may have a bit to do with it."

Danica nodded. "I'm glad. You two seem really good together. As the most senior employee, I'd like Ollie to take on more leadership roles as well."

"Oh god," I winced, "do we have to tell him that? It will go straight to his head."

She laughed again. "We'll keep him grounded, but I think he's got a lot of potential and we don't want to waste that."

"Yeah, I guess." I pretended to be put out. "You just don't understand how annoying he'll get if he finds out you want to give him more responsibility."

"We'll ease him into it slowly. How's that?"

I nodded. "I'm mostly joking. He's smart and really good at his job. He definitely has potential and deserves to move up."

Danica and I said goodbye, and I set the alarm—which was also being reset within the next few days—and headed home.

On the way, I stopped by the flower shop and grocery.

When I got home, Ollie was sitting up in bed, but his eyes were closed.

"Hey," I said softly. "Where's your bed buddy?"

"He just left. I was worried you wouldn't be okay finding me riding another cock," Ollie answered, a grin on his face and not even opening his eyes.

"I meant Leighton," I deadpanned.

"Oh, him? He's in the shower. Finally felt well enough to wash the stink off."

"PS," I said as I walked into his room, "for future

reference, I definitely would not be okay with finding you riding another cock."

Ollie laughed as he opened his eyes. "Noted. Not to worry, this ass is ruined for anyone but you now, baby. You're stuck with me."

I pulled the flowers and a bag of goodies out from behind my back.

His eyes went wide with genuine surprise and appreciation. "For me?"

I shrugged and sat on the edge of his bed. "Figured you deserved a little treat. Wanted this time you got flowers to be because I bought them just for you, not for the whole staff."

"Oh my god, you're so damn sweet." He took the bag. "I won't open this until you're back. Can you put the flowers in water for me? I want them in here so I can see them while I waste away to nothing tomorrow all by my lonesome."

I snorted. "You're not going to waste away to nothing. You can use the alone time to *rest* and let your head heal."

"I'll be so bored and lonely," Ollie whined. "You should take the day off and keep me occupied."

"No way. You'll spend the day trying to seduce me and that doesn't count as rest. You can rest tomorrow. Maybe listen to an audiobook—no screen time yet—or a podcast. And I think Julian said your dad was going to come visit."

I'd known day two of bedrest was going to be the worst.

"The day after, can I go to LuLu's? I talked to her today —PS, she's pissed at you because you didn't call to let her know what was going on and she had to learn it from my dad and me—she wants me to come for lunch and to hang out on her couch." Ollie's eyes twinkled.

I narrowed my gaze at him. "For real? She invited you?"

He pretended to be offended. "Yes. She loves me."

Yeah, LuLu probably was pissed and probably did invite him.

"Hurry and get my flowers in water so I can open my treats," Ollie said.

I got a vase, filled it with water, and arranged the flowers after snipping off the ends of their stems.

"Here you go, princess," I said, placing the vase on the windowsill. "Is this to your specifications?"

"Perfect. Now, what did you get me?" Ollie moved slowly, but got himself situated cross-legged and dug into the bag of goodies. He turned glistening eyes up to me. "This is maybe the nicest thing anyone has ever done for me."

At that moment, I knew I wanted to spend the rest of my life making my guy happy with unexpected treats and gifts.

"It's not that big of a deal," I said.

"Flowers, chocolate milk, butterfly pea flower tea, candy, a candle, and a stuffed bear?" Ollie asked. "It's a whole little treasure and I love every single bit of it. Thank you so much."

"You're welcome." I leaned down and kissed him. "You want a shower?"

"Ohhhh, sexy time," Ollie started.

"No, just a shower."

"But…"

"Oliver."

"You act like saying my name like that will make me *not* think it's sexy time, but hearing you say my name all gruff and strict like is the exact opposite of a turn-off," he said, pouting.

"Do you want a shower or not?"

"Can I sleep in your room? I'll be in my bed all damn day tomorrow."

"Only. Sleep." I cocked my brow and crossed my arms over my chest.

"Yes, Daddy."

I growled and the only thing that kept me from tackling him to the bed and making him pay for that smartass little mouth was the fact he was still hurt.

We took what Ollie deemed *the world's least sexy shower* and I set him up in my bed. I brought him some of the casserole his dad had sent over and we ate in bed with his new candle burning and his little stuffed bear by his side.

I filled him in on everything the police had found out about Elise.

By the time he was ready for more pain medication, Ollie was dragging and I wasn't far behind.

We fell asleep wrapped in each other's arms.

———

TWO WEEKS LATER, Ollie was completely cleared by his doctor—although, he'd been up and around since the third day of his bedrest, but he'd been doing a pretty decent job of taking it easy.

I'd convinced him to start back to work on half days

and that seemed to help with building his stamina back up. He'd had a few headaches over the past couple weeks, but they were easily eased with Tylenol and his doctor said they'd happen less often as he continued to heal.

"What do you boys have planned this weekend?" LuLu asked as we helped her clean up from the dinner she'd made for us. It was a Friday night, but we'd gone over to visit despite having been there Sunday and Wednesday. Ollie absolutely loved LuLu and the feeling was mutual—they'd bonded in a way I hadn't expected, and it was painful to see how much Ollie had missed out on having a mother figure in his life.

Not that Roger and Julian hadn't been great for him. They'd done the best they could in helping him heal and providing him a loving, stable family.

But he'd missed a positive female in his life.

And LuLu was thrilled to step in and help, even all these years later.

I loved watching them together.

It hurt my heart to think Ollie so desperately needed that motherly presence.

But I was grateful he could find it with a woman I considered a mom more than my birth mother.

In a way, I realized I got the fatherly presence I'd missed out on from Roger—who, if I had my way, would one day be my father-in-law, and from the guys. Sure, none of them were dads, and all of them were younger than me, but my found family meant the world to me and they were helping me heal from my past wounds.

"We're spending all weekend in bed," Ollie said, smacking my ass. "Bash has a lot of sexy time to make up for since he wouldn't let me do anything strenuous these last couple weeks."

"Please stop," I asked, pinching the bridge of my nose and knowing he'd just keep going.

"I *tried* to tell him I could blow him while lying down. I even offered to let him just suck me off—all I had to do was lie there—but he refused. Such a rule follower."

LuLu laughed. "Well, you boys should head home and get a start on your weekend. I've got a date with a man who loves horses."

I chuckled. "Isn't that *a meeting with a man about a horse*?"

LuLu grinned. "Nope. It's a date with a man who loves horses. His name is Ned and he owns several racing horses. He's coming over this evening for drinks. If it goes well, we might go to a horse race next weekend."

Well, damn.

Look at my aunt go.

"Be careful," I warned.

"Yeah, you've got pepper spray, right?" Ollie asked, brow furrowing. "Maybe we should stay and meet this *Ned*."

"Nonsense," LuLu said, waving away our concern. "I've already had a friend's grandson on the police force check him out. He's a good man."

"You've got condoms, right?" Ollie asked, hands on hips like a father with his child before a date. "Just because you're both older doesn't mean sexually transmitted infections aren't an issue. For real," he said, his eyes wide, "I read a lot of nursing home type places run rampant with STIs. Safe sex is important. Let Ned show you his horses and *show you his horse*," he said with an exaggerated wink, "but you be sure to wrap that thing before you climb in the saddle."

"Oh my god," I groaned.

LuLu laughed. "Boys, I was eighteen and beyond in the seventies, I know all about safe sex. I'll be careful, promise. Go on, get out of here and have fun."

We walked hand-in-hand toward home.

"I got tested while I was at the doctor. It all came back negative," Ollie said in a rush. "Not that I think we have to go without, it's just that you mentioned it, and since I was there, I did it. It's no big deal if we keep using them." The words spilled from him in a rush.

I dropped his hand and put my arm around him. "I may have done the same thing. Negative. And we're both on PrEP, we should be good."

Ollie grabbed my hand again and tried to pull me down the sidewalk as I laughed. "Oh my god, you just told me I get your bare dick. Why won't you run?"

We finally reached the apartment and took a quick shower together. I left Ollie to finish by himself—prep was more of an individual thing, at least for us—and lit some candles in my room before spreading a towel on the bed.

The candlelight glowed on his freckled skin and I stroked myself in anticipation when Ollie walked into the room and climbed onto the bed. I rolled him to his back and devoured his mouth. "I wanna eat your ass and fill you with my cum," I growled against his lips.

"Fuck, yes, please." Ollie maneuvered himself to straddle my chest, his ass spread right at my face.

The very thought of sliding into him without any

barrier and knowing my load would spill from his hole had my cock leaking and my balls drawing up tight.

Ollie took me into his hot, wet mouth, working me over good with his tongue, as I gripped his ass and buried my face. Tonguing him open, I licked and savored every inch of his hole. Once I'd worked two spit-slick fingers into him, I slapped his ass.

"Get on your back," I demanded.

Ollie scrambled to comply and I smeared his entrance and my shaft with lube.

Lining my cockhead up with his rosy pucker, I pushed into him, nearly busting a nut as his heat gripped my bare cock.

When Ollie would have lifted his legs and let me rail him hard and fast, I dropped to my elbows, bringing our chests together. I kept my rocking hips deliberately slow and gentle, cupping his face, exploring his mouth with my tongue, absorbing his soft whimpers.

Making love to him.

We had all the time in the world for hard and fast.

We had the rest of our lives for fucking.

I needed him to know—needed him to *feel*—how much I loved him.

Cherished him.

Wanted him by my side forever.

When Ollie choked out my name, I thrust into him with more force, never increasing my speed. My tight balls pressed against the cleft of his ass as my orgasm tingled down my spine, ready to be unleashed.

"Jack yourself," I demanded. "Let me watch you come while my cock is buried in your ass."

Ollie readily complied, fisting his dick and stroking as I pushed up on my hands and watched him jerk his throbbing cock.

His release splattered his belly and his ass clenched around my shaft.

Dropping back to my elbows, I hooked my arms under his shoulders and plunged my tongue between his lips as I thrust into his tight heat over and over.

"Fuck, Oliver, gonna come," I murmured against his lips right before my orgasm screamed through me, my load pulsing hot and thick deep in his body.

I collapsed on top of him, both of us breathing heavily.

"Is it weird I'm super turned on by the fact your cum is in my ass? Like, I can't decide if I wanna keep it in there as lube for round two or feel it leak out," Ollie muttered against my ear.

I chuckled, both of us wincing as my spent cock slipped from his ass. "You've been watching too much porn."

"Very likely," Ollie said. "But really, who's to decide how much is too much?"

We were silent for several moments, basking in the blissful haze of orgasm.

"Oh! Remember when I was on bedrest and you said if I followed doctor's orders you'd tell me all about how much you love me. I followed orders to a T and you never gave me my story time."

I rolled to my side and propped myself up on an elbow. "You don't remember it? Maybe the concussion is messing with your memory." I tried to keep a straight face.

"Don't fuck with me," Ollie protested, slapping a hand

against my chest. "You promised. Now that you've dicked me down and dumped your load in my ass, I want my story."

"You are so very crass," I said.

"Yeah, yeah, you love it."

I pressed a kiss to his forehead where his scar was healing nicely. "I do."

Ollie turned to face me, his hand brushing my hair back before moving to take my hand.

I sighed. "I wasn't looking for love. I thought all I wanted was to look the part, play the part, act the part. I know now none of those things ever gave me what I was truly looking for."

"What were you looking for?" Ollie asked.

I went on. "Until I met you, I had no idea. I thought if I had the right look, the right job, the right superficial relationship, I'd have it, or eventually find it. Then you barreled into my life, my own little human wrecking ball, and destroyed me." I kissed him.

"I didn't mean to destroy you," Ollie whispered.

"You destroyed me in the very best way. You knocked down walls and helped me see what was really important, what I really needed. You helped me see past playing a certain part and how to open myself up to what I truly wanted," I explained, not sure my words were adequate.

"And what do you truly want?" Ollie's words were barely audible.

"You, Oliver. All I want—all I need—is you. I think the center can use me for a bit longer than I originally planned. And I can't imagine not living on Cravenwood Block. But, no matter the home, no matter the job, I know the only thing I truly need is you by my side." I brushed a tear from Ollie's cheek.

"I'll make you a deal. You stand by me and I'll stand by you," Ollie said, his words wavering with emotion.

"I like the sound of that."

Love was the last thing I expected after being cheated on, accused of wrong doing, and losing my job.

But love was exactly what I found on Cravenwood Block.

———

ON CRAVENWOOD BLOCK continues with Julian & Shaw—AVAILABLE HERE.

Also by A.D. Ellis

Jett & Leighton: On Cravenwood Block- a steamy, opposites-attract, bisexual-awakening, roommates-to-lovers M/M romance featuring a sexy-as-sin tattoo artist and a fresh, flashy barista with a smile that lights up the room.

Holly Hills Christmas- Holly Hills Christmas is a steamy, feel-good, M/M age-gap holiday romance.

The Perfect Blend- A steamy, M/M age-gap, marriage of convenience, coffee shop romance

Perfect Timing is a steamy, M/M romance with an introverted, demisexual writer and a big, soft teddy bear of a nurse trying to navigate a love they've always dreamed of but most definitely weren't expecting.

Adore (Remington Place 1) is a steamy, age-gap, bi-awakening, dad's best friend M/M romance with a sassy smartass and a sexy silver fox. It's the first book in the Remington Place series and can be read as a stand-alone.

Crave (Remington Place 2) is a steamy, friends-to-lovers, fake relationship M/M romance with a virgin nursing student and a gruff, grumbly construction worker.

Desire (Remington Place 3) is a steamy, age-gap, hurt/comfort M/M romance featuring a heart-of-gold mechanic and a twink who's a lot stronger than he realizes. *Please note: This story has mention of sex trafficking and sexual abuse.*

Yearn (Remington Place 4)- a steamy, enemies-to-lovers, forced proximity M/M romance between two EMS workers who have hated each other for a decade.

Power Struggle is a steamy M/M, age-gap, forced proximity

romance set in a small town. A twenty-year history, rival schools and jobs, and a hotel with only one bed make for a hot and heavy, sweet and sexy, HEA-guaranteed love story.

Take Me Home M/M age-gap, opposites-attract romance with plenty of steam and a scene that will make you appreciate camouflage and work boots

Let Love In M/M age-gap, forced proximity, dad's best friend, bisexual-awakening romance. Available on AUDIO!

Let Love Win M/M brother's best friend romance. Available on AUDIO!

Buried Secrets Romantic suspense stand-alone title. Available on AUDIO!

Silver in the City (3 books- meet the Silver crew you read about in Forged in the City) Available on AUDIO!

Forged in the City (3 books- a spin-off series from Silver in the City) Available on AUDIO

The BJ Boys Series (3 books, small town, big love) Available on AUDIO

Forever Better Together (friends to lovers) Available on AUDIO!

His Reluctant Cowboy (age gap, opposites attract, cowboy romance) Available on AUDIO!

What Blooms Beneath (LGBT Fantasy romance) Available on AUDIO!

Sawyer

(this was the first M/M I wrote and you may remember Sawyer and Luke being mentioned in Barrett & Ivan as well as in Ryker & Gavin)

————

The Something About Him series has been revamped with revised stories, updated blurbs, and spiffy new covers.

The series is available on ALL of your favorite book platforms!

Bryan & Jase

Brody & Nick

Barrett & Ivan

Braeton & Drew

Ryker & Gavin

Kade & Cameron

———

A.D.'s first stories (all male/female except <u>Sawyer</u> which is male/male) are in the Torey Hope and Torey Hope: The Later Years series. Find the 8 book box set HERE or you can find each individual title on Amazon.

For Nicky

Because of Beckett

Christmas in Torey Hope

Loving Josie

Decker

Sawyer

Zach

Kendrick

About the Author

A.D. Ellis is an Indiana girl, born and raised. She spends much of her time in central Indiana as an instructional coach/teacher in the inner city of Indianapolis, being a mom to two amazing teenagers, and wondering how she and her husband of over two decades haven't driven each other insane yet. A lot of her time is also devoted to phone call avoidance and her hatred of cooking.

She loves chocolate, wine, pizza, and naps along with reading and writing romance. These loves don't leave much time for housework, much to the chagrin of her husband. Who would pick cleaning the house over a nap or a good book? She uses any extra time to increase her fluency in sarcasm.

A.D. uses she/they pronouns.

Sign up at http://www.subscribepage.com/ADEllisNewsMMRomance for a FREE books!

Website http://adellisauthor.com/

Find me EVERYWHERE at https://www.adellisauthor.com/mylinks/

Connect with A.D. Ellis

Follow my website http://www.adellisauthor.com or find me on Facebook

http://www.facebook.com/adellisauthor

If you want to get updates about releases, interviews, sales, giveaways, and more please sign up for my newsletter http://www.subscribepage.com/ADEllisNewsMMRomance

Check out my TikTok- https://www.tiktok.com/@adellisauthor

You can also find me on Twitter http://www.twitter.com/ADEllisAuthor

Find me on Spotify if you'd like to listen to the playlist for this book (mainly just the songs I listened to while writing). Just search for A.D. Ellis.

To make it easy, find me EVERYWHERE here- https://www.adellisauthor.com/mylinks/

Acknowledgments

It's always so hard to write this part because I'm worried I'll forget someone without meaning to.

Readers- you are the reason I write. As long as you continue reading my stories, I'll continue writing them. Thank you for your support.

Bloggers- your support, reviews, and promotion are very much appreciated. Thank you!

My author buddies- I don't know that I could keep doing this without our brainstorm sessions, laughter, road trips, meals, wine, and friendship as my support.

Thank you to my alpha readers, betas, editors, proofreaders, and ARC readers! Your eyes and input are beyond important to me.

Brett and Gage- as usual, I doubt you even grasp how much your support, input, and friendship mean to me. This author journey has brought many wonderful things into my life, and you both are two of the BEST! I'm blessed to call you friends.

My family and friends- thank you for your love and support, always.

Copyright © 2022 by A.D. Ellis

All rights reserved.

No part of this book may be reproduced in any form or by any electronic or mechanical means, including information storage and retrieval systems, without written permission from the author, except for the use of brief quotations in a book review. The characters in this book are entirely fictional. Any resemblance to actual persons living or dead is entirely coincidental.